I0630896

# LILLIE

## By

INTERNATIONAL BESTSELLING AUTHOR

# MYA O' MALLEY

Lillie

By Mya O'Malley

www.myaomalley.com

ISBN-13: 978-0-9978596-5-2
ISBN-10: 0-9978596-5-2

Cover Art by P.S. Cover Design
Formatting by Jill Sava, Love Affair With Fiction

*For Alexandra*

# PROLOGUE

SHE WOKE, TREMBLING from the same dream she had experienced nearly every night lately–only this time it had a unique twist–this time she survived.

It should be getting easier; you would think so, at least. But no, how could Naomi erase the horrific images of when Nick had placed her in that dark, distant realm, trapped in the cold, dank earth?

In real life she had survived. Of course she had, she was lying here, snug and safe next to Bryce, who'd slept through this latest nightmare, blissfully unaware of the graphic images that floated so freely in her head. Images that may creep to the recesses of her thoughts at times, but would never truly leave her mind. Maybe the fact that she had lived in this version of the dream meant the nighttime visions would disappear–poof, gone–just like that. Naomi stifled a bitter laugh. If only.

Now, she needed to let go. Naomi had her life to get on with, and besides, all of the spirits from her past had been served their justice, received their peaceful endings. So then what was up with this incessant, smothering, recurring nightmare?

If only she could get her own blissful ending and remove the horrific memories of her past battle with the spirit of her ex boyfriend, Nick. After all, they had made peace with one another, so the consistent nagging of the dream should be long gone.

"Hey," Bryce mumbled, pulling Naomi closer. She shut her eyes, attempting to allow only clean, pure thoughts to enter. She focused on him–her senses basked in Bryce. Just Bryce. He pulled her closer still, gently reaching for her as she touched the rough stubble on his cheek. There. This seemed to be working.

Naomi got her reprieve as she drew Bryce's mouth toward hers.

# CHAPTER ONE

SHE SWEPT THE cobwebs to the side with her dusty fingertips. She brushed her hands along the shiver of goose bumps rushing up and down her arms. Why wouldn't Bryce have mentioned this unique treasure that lay beyond the walls of their house? How could he have possibly forgotten to tell her?

*Her,* of all people?

Unless he didn't know.

Naomi supposed Bryce could be unaware of the hidden path that wound itself from the bottom floor to the top. She, however, would have scoured every inch of this relic of a home hours upon moving in, which she realized with newfound curiosity, that she was only getting around to now.

Better late than never. Reaching for her cell phone, Naomi powered it on and scrambled to find the flashlight app.

Here we go. "This is ridiculously cool." Naomi breathed the words into the empty crevices of the walls.

Her eyes widened as she took in the dark, curving stairway with bare walls. The stone and brick style Dutch Colonial house was built in the late 1700's. This had to be one of those secret passageways, like the ones Revolutionary War soldiers or runaway slaves must have tucked themselves away in, fearing for their lives as they relied on sheer courage, powerful dreams of a possible future, one far better than what they had experienced, and little else to guide them. Hard to imagine that at one time, people had to hide away within these dim, musty walls, thankfully, there had been brave souls that had assisted these people, giving them a chance at a fresh, new beginning.

Naomi reminded herself to stay focused as she recalled the reason she had uncovered this gem in the first place.

Soft moaning, or was that whining? But honestly–it could just be her vivid imagination working overtime.

The latter was most definitely a possibility. Scratch that, a strong probability.

Given Naomi's past encounters, it was no wonder she had ghosts on her mind. Naomi lived, breathed, and slept the paranormal. To her, the unearthly spirits that seemed destined to find her were as natural as breathing. She seemed to possess some kind of magnetic pull that summoned the otherworldly spirits.

Problem was, since Naomi's wedding and recent move into Bryce's house, now her own home as well, things had been strangely quiet on the paranormal front. All Naomi had prayed for, for months prior when she was knee-deep in ghosts, was peace and quiet, a break from the spirits who so desperately sought her out, begging her to save their souls while swallowing up her energy, focus, and time spent on nurturing her relationship with Bryce.

Her only wish now was to settle in with Bryce and her stepdaughter, Holly. Tunnel vision with ghosts as her sole focus had made it difficult to practice any sense of normalcy.

Aside from the relentless nightmares, Naomi was happy now. She worked from home, writing her novels. A huge perk was that she could be home for Holly when she got off the bus each day after school. Lately, her books had mimicked reality and the paranormal realm as her real-life focus had been putting unsettled spirits to rest. As a matter of fact, her current work in progress centered around the conflicted spirit of Nick. It was easy to write about her own experiences, even if it brought back all of the turmoil and horror she had experienced while trying to solve the mystery surrounding Nick's demise. Naomi wondered if she would have hit bestseller status had the ghost of Maggie never graced Naomi with her presence.

All the pieces of her life with Bryce and Holly had been coming together. Placing her home, just down the small dirt road, up for sale had been bittersweet. Now with the move made, and the new owner settled in at her old place, it was time to relax and just take a breather. A faint grin played across her face at the thought of her new neighbor.

Problem was, now that she had her wish, she found herself overreacting at the slightest movement, the smallest sound. Bryce would laugh at her, of course. He knew Naomi all too well, understood that she was closely tied to those spirits that she had helped in the past. He understood that a small part of Naomi almost seemed incomplete without them. So it made sense that she had poked around at the walls, looking for trouble.

Nothing seemed out of place or unusual though, now that she was deep inside the heart of the house. The fact that nothing was amiss didn't mean that Naomi still couldn't enjoy the chance to explore.

Coughing at the feel of a tickle of dust in her lungs, Naomi composed herself then shone the light from her phone toward the ceiling. How many people had traveled these stairs? One? Many? Did they survive? She closed her eyes for the briefest of moments, clearing her mind to open herself up to the space before her and the unknown secrets it held.

A sudden wave of sadness hit Naomi–hard. She easily tuned into the emotions of those around her, an *empath*, it was termed. More like *soaked* into people and their problems, she figured.

This time was no different, even considering that her melancholy was now most likely tied to events from many, many years ago. It didn't matter though, for time was merely a riddle to solve, another dimension to break through. Naomi had touched several departed souls. Souls from the recent past. With a tinge of anticipation, Naomi wondered what it would be like to sync with an ancient soul...if it was possible for her to connect with someone hundreds of years old. With a wide grin, she grasped hold of the thought and quickly turned it to hope. Bryce would be pissed if he knew she lingered within the walls of their home, contemplating the desire to start up trouble once more.

Straining to hear even the slightest movement, Naomi grew impatient as she suddenly lost her connection. It was just her now, alone in that dark space. She closed her eyes once more, trying to bring forth the emotions that had come to her so easily moments before. What had hit her earlier now proved elusive. She sighed, but continued up the stairs, despite the chill in the air.

There. She had reached the top floor, and, if she figured it right, Naomi thought the crawl space that stood before her was most likely on the other side of the wall in the guest bedroom. It was no wonder she had never discovered the passageway, for the broad armoire in the room had done a fine job of covering up this delicious little gem of a secret. The furniture had come with the house when Bryce had been renting it, so it made sense that he had never encountered the spot where the passageway came to its end.

Pushing with all her strength against the wall, Naomi huffed before wiping the dust from her hands. The wall wouldn't budge. There was nothing else to see here and it was getting late. She would return another time. She forced her mind from the notion of needy ancient spirits, knowing that Bryce and Holly were expecting her downstairs.

Her own footsteps were the only sound as Naomi traveled down to the bottom floor. A faint slice of light from the small doorway below allowed Naomi to swiftly work her way down. The familiar blur of black fur swept past the light as Zelda, Naomi's pitch-black cat, announced her presence with a shrill cry.

A chill swept over Naomi as things began to happen all at once. She knew Zelda all too well and the sadness that touched her before came back with a punch. Naomi gasped for air and bent down to compose herself as the cat's shrieks grew louder. Zelda had been known to spook, but not easily. Like Naomi, the cat also had plenty of experience with spirits–nearly as much as she, herself, had. Naomi actually considered her feline to be an expert of sorts when it came to detecting spirits. Imagine that.

Naomi took in a fresh gulp of air and braced herself. Not knowing what she would find when she spun her head around, she swallowed hard, her eyes open wide.

Nothing.

Nothing but deafening silence hit Naomi's sensitive ears. This spirit seemed to slam her hard and fast with emotion, and then pull back just as quickly, almost as if he or she were playing with her, tricks of the mind. All was quiet now, but if she concentrated just a bit more, she was sure she would uncover the reason for Zelda's behavior.

*Concentrate. Concentrate.*

Yes—there it was. This time she couldn't mistake the sound. Someone or something wept, the faint moans reaching Naomi softly in the diminishing light.

Naomi tuned into the emotion, attempting to pinpoint the source. Female. Yes, this appeared to be a female voice, but there was something different than what she was accustomed to. Something wasn't fitting, it was about the tone, the pitch of the cries. Naomi covered her ears with trembling hands and, against her will, she felt herself sucked in—into a place far worse than what she had ever experienced before. She heard the continued weeping, closing her eyes.

She soon discovered that there was an emotion far worse than fear—it was sorrow.

Naomi opened her eyes briefly, because the images in her own head were intolerable, but closed them once more because she needed to be certain. Needed to be sure the familiar face was who or what she thought it was.

*No.*

But there was no denying what faced her, occupying not just her mind, but every inch of her body. Naomi stood face to face with the image of her childhood dreams and nightmares. How she'd blocked this out, she didn't know, for now she stood before the nagging, dark soul of a child she had met many, many times before.

Naomi placed a hand on her thumping chest. The girl conjured up fear with every distant memory filtering through her mind. Like playing cards being flipped, each second revealed a new source of terror.

No one had believed her as a child when she'd thought this young girl was her imaginary friend, and no one had believed her when the same girl haunted her dreams until just before adolescence. Eventually, the girl had seemed to lose interest in taunting Naomi, begging her to perform the naughtiest of tasks, all of which Naomi firmly stood her ground against. What kind of child would ask another to trip her own mother, say mean spirited comments to her parents?

Naomi hadn't questioned her disappearance, for she had only been relieved at the silence that the child's absence had left. She had assumed the spirit had moved on to torture another–she hadn't counted on the fact that perhaps the child hadn't given up on her at all, maybe she was just biding her time, waiting all these years for just the right time to pounce again, this time perhaps with more ammunition.

She had forgotten all about her–her mind had protected a young Naomi from the horror, but unfortunately, Naomi now remembered. She remembered every last detail, and with that, she also knew why she had chosen to forget.

# CHAPTER TWO

"HERE YOU GO." Holly smiled widely as she placed a small chocolate chip cookie on the napkin beside her own.

Naomi had walked right past Holly. She was still reeling from the blast from her past minutes earlier. Ellie, yes, that's what she used to call her little *friend*. Ellie. Naomi placed a hand on her stomach, attempting to calm her tumultuous belly.

*Finally, having Holly's words sink in, she backed up and gazed upon the scene before her.*

"Oh, I'm sorry. Is that for me?" Naomi ran a hand through her tangle of dark hair.

"No, silly. This is for my friend." Holly shook her head, her smooth brown hair spilling over her tiny shoulders. And at that, Holly went right on, continuing her conversation with the empty space beside her. A chill coursed through Naomi, pulsing into her body. She needed to sit and still her quaking knees.

So this is what Bryce was referring to. He had mentioned Holly's imaginary friend the other night. Naomi assured Bryce that this behavior was typical for a young child, especially an only child like Holly. And, as Naomi had pointed out to Bryce, the fact that Holly had recently lost her mother, certainly added to her reasoning. Sure, Holly was now seven years old, but she had been through so much. Holly's mom had been a pain in the butt, both in life and in death. At least that's what she had explained away to Bryce.

Could it be that Ellie had taken hold of Holly? Forcing her friendship on her just as she had done to Naomi so long ago? She preyed on the innocent, that's what Ellie thrived on, or maybe it *was* simply an imaginary friend, due to the many changes in Holly's life.

Naomi shivered as she took a steady breath. Ghosts– God, so many ghosts. She recalled her experience with the ghost of Genna, Holly's mother. Genna had wreaked havoc on her relationship with Bryce. They had not known at the time that Genna had actually been killed by the hands of an abusive boyfriend. Alas, life can be stranger than fiction, Naomi soon found out, as her own ex, Nick, used Genna in a battle against Naomi, attempting to draw a wedge between her and Bryce.

It was all old news though, and she and Bryce had survived, their love stronger as a result.

Her eyes wandered back to the empty space beside Holly. Deciding to press the matter a bit, Naomi placed her hands on the table in front of her. "Can I join you? You and…"

"Naomi, I call her Lillie, and I'm not sure that she would be comfortable with you staying."

*Ellie. Lillie.*

The names were so close to one another. Could it be?

Naomi closed her eyes, hearing a voice that had visited her too many times during her childhood.

*Not Ellie. Lillie. It's Lillie. Say it—Lillie!*

That's right—she had never been able to get that name right and it had pissed the little ghost off to no end. Of course it was her, there was no other feasible explanation for the thickness of the air back in the passageway. She was *here*.

Lillie was *here*, right now, in their house.

"Oh, I see." She sat back and watched as Holly shook her head, mumbling to the empty chair. Naomi's mind whirred with possible solutions to ridding this house of the young spirit, but anything sensible eluded her right now.

"It's okay, Naomi. She said you can stay."

"Oh did she now?" Naomi's eyes narrowed, but she complied and remained in the chair across from Holly. She needed a breather—a chance to step back and try to figure out what to do next.

"Naomi?"

She glanced up and studied Holly. Her stepdaughter was growing to be a young lady before her eyes. Naomi recalled, just months ago, when Holly would lovingly refer to her as *Nomi*. Now, Holly considered herself to be much wiser to the world around her and therefore spoke Naomi's name with perfect pronunciation. Sometimes Holly would also refer to Naomi as *Mommy*. The last thing Naomi wanted was to confuse the girl, so as far as Naomi was concerned, she could address her any way she desired.

"What? What is it, honey?"

"She wants to know if you like her name." A smug smile set on Holly's lips, almost as if she knew that Naomi was also familiar with this imaginary friend of hers. But there was no way she could know unless Lillie had decided to tell her. "She would like to hear you say it."

Of course she would. Half tempted to call her Ellie, Naomi swallowed and did as was requested. "Lillie-it um– it's a beautiful name, like the flower." Naomi nodded as she spoke to the chair beside her.

"No, it's not spelled the same. Her name is Lillian. It's her nickname, L-i-l-l-i-e, and she doesn't feel pretty like a flower," Holly huffed.

"I see." Naomi covered her eyes, attempting to ward off the pounding in her head. She vaguely recalled similar comments from when she, herself, was a child. Naomi managed to keep a sliver of a smile on her face as she opened her eyes. "Why does your friend feel she isn't pretty? I'm sure she is–" Did she remember any more offbeat comments about that from her own childhood? She strained her brain, but there was so much that was fuzzy–too many foggy details.

"Stop! Lillie said just stop placating her." Holly faced her, eyes cold.

Sitting back in her seat, Naomi placed her hand over her chest. Placating her?

For lack of a better option, Naomi decided it was time to change the subject. "What do you say we figure out what's for dinner tonight, okay?" Naomi leaned over to gently place her hand on Holly's wrist.

Pulling her hand back, Holly sighed deeply. "You don't like her, do you?"

"I–why would you say that?"

"She knows how you feel. Lillie is actually very nice, but she has her secrets."

Naomi cleared her throat and mindlessly gobbled down the small cookie in front of her.

Secrets? Had she been privy to Lillie's secrets way back when? The more she strained to remember, the harder it became.

Holly then stood to retrieve another cookie for her new friend. Placing a napkin on the table, Holly sat back down to eat her cookie. The chatter continued, but Naomi had no earthly idea what Holly rambled on about.

All she could wonder about was why Lillie was here–in their house, in the passageway.

No wonder she had blocked the girl and the dreams from her mind. Ellie or Lillie, or whoever she was, was from long ago it seemed–long, long, ago. Trapped within the walls of a house, she remembered that now. Presumably, it must be this house–nothing else made sense. She would sort out the logistics later. But wait–there were others. Yes–other voices she had heard as a child. There had been adults and other younger voices, too. Crying, weeping, then screaming.

Over and over.

Over and over.

Over and over.

Somehow, Naomi managed to concentrate on the rest of the conversation between Holly and Lillie. Holly now muttered on about dolls and a game called Potsie.

She remembered hearing somewhere that the term referred to the game of Hopscotch. Naomi had first assumed the old-fashioned game of Hopscotch she had once played in her own childhood must be making a comeback. Now, she knew better. Holly had asked Bryce just the other day to sketch out the squares for the game on their driveway. Each day after school now, it was the first thing Holly asked to play, after her snack. Before she could clear her mind from the game of Potsie, Holly intruded with a harsh command.

"Okay, Lillie said it's time for you to leave." Holly waved her arm dramatically through the air, dismissing her, just like that.

Parenting had the tendency to be tricky when to came to Holly. For the most part, her stepdaughter behaved sweetly and used her manners. Did the circumstances around this rudeness excuse her? Yes, this was different, but still. Since the death of Genna though, Naomi could see that the little girl had a lot on her mind, and at times, it showed with her precocious, albeit recent, snippy attitude.

"You know, Holly–it really isn't polite to ask me to leave," Naomi began.

"*I* didn't ask you to leave. *She* did. Don't get mad at me." Holly's gaze drifted to the empty chair beside her as she huffed and drew her arms across her chest.

Naomi swallowed, unsure of her next move.

"What's this about asking Naomi to leave?" Bryce's voice hitched a notch.

Naomi nearly jumped at the sound of his voice coming from behind her. She turned to face Bryce. He must have slipped in while her mind was wrapped around all of this insanity.

"It's nothing, Bryce–really, it's fine." And she was sure it would be–well, almost sure.

"I don't know what's going on around here, but from where I stand, it looks like you owe Naomi an apology, young lady."

Blowing a piece of hair from her eyes, Holly mumbled a brief apology, her gaze still fixed on the spot next to her.

"I'm sorry, I didn't quite hear that."

"Sorry, Mommy."

Naomi melted at the name Naomi chose to address her

with. See? It would be fine. "Bryce, I can handle this." She leaned over and whispered in his ear.

Holly lifted her face, focusing in on Naomi. "Lillie says it's not polite to whisper."

"Lillie?" Bryce's mouth turned down, his eyes darted from Holly to Naomi.

Tightening her hold on Bryce's arm, Naomi choked back a gasp. One thing seemed evident here–if she were right, and this was, in fact, Lillie, the spirit she had also dealt with in the past, she sure as heck didn't seem to like her old friend now. Naomi wasn't sure the spirit had even liked her back then, and the thought did nothing to comfort her. She released her grip on Bryce and then wrapped her arms across her chest.

"What's going on here?"

"Drop it."

Naomi's jaw dropped at the harsh words, they sounded so wrong coming out of Holly's mouth.

This wasn't Holly. This couldn't be the little girl who smiled openly, soaking up attention from Naomi.

"Excuse me, young lady?" Bryce knelt down so that he faced Holly eye to eye.

"Sorry, Daddy. Sorry, *Mommy*."

Naomi swore Holly's eyes challenged her as she now spoke the title with an edge of attitude. As quickly as it had come on, though, Holly's gaze then glazed over, becoming replaced once again by innocent, sweet brown eyes.

If Bryce noticed the shift in her gaze, he hadn't reacted. "I don't ever want to hear you speak that way again, not to Naomi and not to anyone. Understand?" Holly bobbed her chin up and down.

"And I asked who Lillie is."

Instead of a harsh command, this time Holly simply

turned away and ignored her father.

"Holly!" Bryce's eyes moved from Holly and then to Naomi, in a desperate plea for help.

Naomi bit her lip and clenched her hands. She needed to speak with Bryce in the worst way, but this conversation was best saved for when Naomi had a chance to speak with Bryce alone.

"She said to *drop it*!" The words shot out of Holly's mouth in a flash. And this time Bryce couldn't have missed the defiant flash in Holly's eyes. He leaned closer, mouth open.

"No. Just—just give her a minute." Naomi clutched onto his arm, her chest thumping.

It was brief-so quick in fact, that Naomi couldn't honestly swear she had seen it. Was that a dark shadow right beside Holly? In the blink of her eyes, all appeared normal. But that feeling—that nagging inner voice told her to beware.

Naomi considered the old adage—be careful what you wish for. That tiny piece inside of Naomi that yearned for her connection to the spirit world may have gotten what she desired.

SHE WINCED, BITING at her lip as Bryce fell back into the all too familiar act of pacing the floors. If she had worried him for no reason, she felt awful, but the near certainty that Holly's new friend was her Ellie was a feeling Naomi couldn't shake. What worried her most was knowing how spiteful and vengeful the little ghost could be.

"This is crazy. Crazy, do you hear me?"

Naomi simply nodded and held her tongue.

"It can't be. You're wrong here, Naomi. Everything was fine here, we never had any problems before, until–well…" Bryce expelled a bitter laugh, locking his eyes on her.

She couldn't hold back because now she felt that rush of irritation moving her forward. "Go ahead, Bryce. Say it." She crossed her arms around her chest, waiting him out. He was just about to say it, the words had nearly spilled from his mouth.

"Until *I* moved in." She provided the words that he couldn't seem to summon the courage to speak.

Need she remind him that Genna's ghost had indeed made a visit or two to Holly's bedroom? Had he conveniently forgotten that piece of information?

"That's not how I meant it."

"Oh?"

"No, this is ridiculous. She's going through a rebellious streak, that's *it*. She just lost her mother not too long ago. You said it yourself."

Naomi swallowed and considered her next words carefully. "*Okay*, but things have changed. I *saw* her, *heard* her myself in the hidden stairway. You can't dismiss this. I mean, with everything I've been through–everything *we've* been through. I *felt* Lillie to my very core within those walls. When am I ever wrong about these things?"

"Geez-now we're calling this figment of imagination by a name? Lillie?" His eyes went wide. "No–no. This can't be happening again. I won't even allow my head to go there. You freed them all, you sent them all to better places."

He avoided eye contact with her and she cringed at his desperation. Maybe she should have kept her accusations to herself until she had solid proof. But she knew.

She *knew.*

Finally, his gaze penetrated her. "Naomi, don't take this the wrong way, but have you considered that maybe you *want* this? Maybe you thrive on this and that you could be wrong?"

*Thrive on it?* That was a bit dramatic. "Excuse me? Do you think I *enjoyed* being stalked by the evil spirit of my psycho ex-boyfriend?"

He shrugged and seemed to consider it. "Well, maybe not *him,* but what about Maggie and Ryan?"

"Are you kidding me?" But her voice hitched, and she broke their gaze.

He moved closer until he was standing inches from her face. "You enjoyed it, maybe just a little bit." He squeezed his fingers together, purposely, with stubborn determination. "Admit it, Naomi. They give you purpose."

She opened her mouth to respond but then closed it tightly.

Damn him.

They *did.* The ghosts did give her a sort of purpose she supposed, and they made her feel unique, special. What was wrong with that?

Hadn't she just longed for some part of her that was missing? But *this?* No, she definitely did not want Holly involved in her walks on the dark side. Damn.

"You—you're probably right, to a certain extent that is." She felt her emotions rising and clamped them down tight, shutting off her frustration. Her eyes moistened as she gazed up at him. "But this has the potential to be different from the others, Bryce."

His eyes darted, making brief contact with her, and then he turned away.

"Bryce." She reached out a hand to touch him. His flinch didn't go unnoticed, but she continued, "Bryce? I would never want to involve Holly in any way. You have to believe that. I would never ask for *this.*"

Still, he remained silent. Not sure what to expect, Naomi reached over anyway and wrapped her arms around him, feeling the thump of his chest on hers. He allowed her to hold him for a brief moment before he broke their embrace.

"I won't allow her to be hurt." His steady gaze bore into her. "Under any circumstances. If this is true, I'll do whatever is within my power to stop it."

The finality of his words gave her pause. How could they stop this? Bryce was a strong man, but she knew his expertise in dealing with the paranormal was quite limited. Hell, she wasn't even betting on herself being able to control this one. Lillie, she felt, would prove to be a challenge.

Holding herself steady, she let her thoughts wander back to his accusation that she had asked for this. Hadn't she dreamed of Maggie and Ryan just last night? They made regular appearances while she slept, along with that hellish nightmare of Nick and the terror of what he had put her through.

These spirits were so engrained in her own being that it was becoming impossible to detach them from her thoughts, even in slumber. They all seemed to hold a piece of her, grabbing at her, demanding attention, even still.

But if she was going to be honest with herself, she knew they were also a part of what defined her, a part of what made her such a talented writer, a part of who she was, and it seemed there wasn't a damn thing she could do about it but wait for them to come to her.

# CHAPTER THREE

THE QUIET WALK between their houses allowed Naomi a moment of peace. She gazed out at the trees with their smattering of orange and red hues, and of course, to the small graveyard beyond. One of her favorite things about this property was the fact that the only two houses on the tranquil, dead end street were the one she shared with Bryce, which stood at the end of the drive, and her old home.

Her old place looked exactly the same from the outside, save the new welcome mat and small garden on the side of the house. Her gaze lingered on the small lot across from her old home and memories of Ryan surfaced. She thought of all the times Ryan had parked his truck there and a familiar warm feeling swept through her.

The cemetery that edged the property from behind still appeared as it always had–creepy, but also hauntingly inviting and irresistible to her writer's mind. She missed her old Saltbox 1700's house, but knew that her new home held just as much history and enough intrigue to keep her occupied.

She knew her imagination differed from most and that any normal person would be petrified to live practically on the grounds of the graveyard beyond. The spots where Maggie and Ryan were laid to rest were on the far end and Nick rested up the path a bit further. All of her desperate souls were undeniably close–so very near, both in distance and in her heart.

Even Nick had eventually grown on her. He certainly hadn't been one of her fondest people in life, but her troubled ex-boyfriend had redeemed himself not only by realizing his weaknesses, but by seeking out her love and forgiveness, which she had finally given him at the end of their long, horrific ordeal.

Naomi wished she could see these precious souls whenever she wished, but it seemed when all was right with the world, they rested, settled into the peace. The only appearances made were in her dreams, and Naomi wasn't sure if they were just that–dreams, or maybe more. She liked to believe they came to her when she was fast asleep, checking in to let Naomi know they were still connected.

It still felt strange to be a visitor in her old home, she thought, as she raised her hand to rap on the door. Naomi smiled as it opened in a matter of seconds.

"Good morning." She was led into the kitchen. Glancing around, Naomi smelled the coffee before she spotted the pot. "How is it that you can look so amazing this early in the morning?" It was something she had been saying to her friend since they had become close.

"Oh, please." And as usual, Miriam waved a dismissive

hand to banish the compliment. Officer Miriam Marty didn't take compliments well. Her humble friend had experienced her share of pain and heartache and maintained a tough exterior.

"How are you settling in?" Naomi's gaze scanned around her friend's cozy home, her heart filling with warmth for one of her favorite places. When Naomi had placed her house up for sale, she had been surprised that Miriam was interested in buying it. Miriam's lease was up on the condo she rented across town, and she seemed ready to start a new chapter in her life after all the business with her ex-boyfriend Phil and his harsh betrayal.

Naomi could only sell to someone who would cherish and appreciate her old home nearly as much as she had. Miriam had always loved this place, and that made Naomi's move up the short road much easier.

Naomi's hope was that this place would serve to heal Miriam's soul. She knew better than to bring up the subject of Miriam's ex. Phil was serving his life sentence in maximum security. Besides murdering Nick, Phil also had attempted murder attached to his sentence. She still cringed thinking of how close he had come to killing her that day, not so long ago, when he realized Naomi had uncovered his secrets.

"Well, so far all is good. And quiet." Miriam chuckled slightly as her eyes glanced around the room. "I half expected this house to be filled with ghosts, but—it seems now that you're gone, there's nothing funny going on here."

That didn't surprise Naomi. "Yeah, well. They seem to have a thing for following me I guess."

"Ain't that the truth. But hey, now that everything is settled, you can finally relax. That must feel good, even to you." Miriam's skeptical eyes met hers.

"Yeah, sure." Naomi reached into the cabinet above the sink where she had once kept her own coffee mugs and found one of Miriam's favorites.

"Go ahead, help yourself," Miriam chuckled as Naomi filled her cup.

Naomi would have usually kept the banter going, but instead, she remained quiet as her thoughts stayed on Miriam's comment.

"So, how's life over there with your amazing little family?" Miriam's eyes met hers from behind her steaming mug.

Naomi offered up a half smile as she returned her attention to pouring some milk into her coffee. "Great. He's wonderful–they both are." But her voice drifted off, and it wasn't lost on Miriam.

"Everything okay?" Miriam's voice rose in concern.

Opening her mouth to speak, Naomi thought better and merely shook her head. She had come here for a break. She didn't wish to rehash her worries.

"Of course."

"If you say so."

She nodded as her gaze remained fixed on the kitchen table before her. Then she remembered that although a change of scenery was needed, there was also another purpose for her visit to Miriam's house.

"You said you wanted to talk to me about something?"

Miriam eyed her over the rim of her cup. "How's your novel going?"

Naomi had met her publishing deadlines and was planning on self-publishing her current work in progress: Nick's story. This allowed her some freedom in terms of timelines. Mixing traditional publishing with her own projects gave her a bit more flexibility, something she could certainly use with the recent past events.

"Well, you know I don't like to talk too much about my books until they're finished, but so far, so good. Why do you ask?"

"I was wondering if you had some free time in your schedule."

She squinted at her friend. "Why?"

"I have this case. It's a tough one."

It had to be a challenging one if Miriam actually admitted it. This grabbed Naomi's interest. "And?"

"*And*...I figured with all of your, well–you know, talent, that your insight might be helpful."

She nearly spit out the coffee she had just sipped. "Are you, Officer Miriam Marty, actually asking for help?" This was a first.

"Don't do that." But Miriam's grin spread as she couldn't contain herself.

"Say it. Say you need me, Miriam. I have to hear the words I thought I'd never hear."

"Shut the hell up." Miriam flicked the spoon on the table in Naomi's direction with a smirk.

"Fine, fine. What's this all about?" She sat on the edge of her chair, leaning toward Miriam.

"Okay, a woman discovered a body in the old abandoned hospital, the one in Bloomview."

Naomi knew the one. The property housed an entire mental health facility that had been closed down many years earlier. The place was built some time during the mid to late 1800's and was beyond creepy in Naomi's opinion. Strange thing was that you had to drive past the dilapidated structures in order to reach the newer, working facility, which served as an outpatient rehabilitation center.

"What was this woman even doing inside?"

"Besides trespassing, she was taking photos. It seems that the old hospital is a favorite spot for amateur photographers. Who knew? She told me she's been in there many times. She even showed me the pictures. I have to say, she has talent." Miriam wiggled her brows.

"Hm. Okay, so where do I come into this?" Naomi's overactive mind was already there, imagining dark, empty spaces, the musty smells and broken windows. Not to mention rats and an abundance of insects.

"The body, the deceased, was a woman. Autopsy pegged her to be mid-thirties or so—but no solid suspects, no motive." Miriam sighed. "The photographer stumbled upon the body the morning after she passed."

"Cause of death?"

"Wounds on her neck. She was strangled."

Naomi's mind bent around various scenarios in which this woman could have ended up in the old building.

"Was she homeless?"

"No, and as a matter of fact, she lived near us and was recently separated."

Recently separated and strangled to death. The obvious rang out in her head, but of course Miriam would have gone over the possibility of the estranged husband as a suspect.

"You know that strangulation usually means—"

"I know, I know. We checked the husband and he has a solid alibi. Claims he was on a date with a woman he met online."

"Were they in a public place?"

"Yup. A fancy Italian restaurant across the river. I spoke with the manager and the waiter who served them. The couple ran up a steep bill and consumed large quantities of very expensive red wine."

"And the determined time of death was confirmed? I mean, could the murder have taken place a few hours before?"

"He has an alibi for nearly every moment of the day, from the time he showed up at work, to the stop at the gas station, florist, and pharmacy."

"Sounds like this guy had a pretty busy day. Could he have purposely set up the various stops throughout the day to cover his tracks?"

"You know as much as I do."

This was her friend's most recent overused phrase, and she knew it irked Naomi every time she used it.

"I hate it–"

"I know." Miriam smirked as she reached for her mug.

"What's her name?"

"Sharon Wilde of Shoreham Falls. She'd been doing some dating of her own since her recent separation, and I have to tell you, the guy she just started dating appears genuinely distraught. Either that, or he's a very good actor."

"So you do know more than me."

Miriam winked, and then rose from the table and reached for a box of muffins. "Want one?"

"No, I'm good. So where does this leave me? I mean, I can only communicate with certain spirits, ones that need me. I don't think I could really help."

"It can't hurt. Listen, we've exhausted all of our resources, and I just got to thinking that maybe if you took a look at her, maybe peruse the crime scene, you might pick up on something."

"Sure, why not? I guess it couldn't hurt. I'm all yours."

"I was hoping you'd say that. Let's go."

Was she serious? "Right now?"

"No time like the present. Finish your coffee, let's go."

Bossy. Her friend was downright bossy. "Yes, ma'am." She swigged down the rest of her coffee and stood to follow Miriam out the door.

"And Naomi?" Miriam turned to face her once they were outside. "I *will* find out what's wrong with you."

"What are you talking about?"

"I'm not an idiot. Something's up with you, and don't try to tell me differently."

There was no point in denying it. "Fine. It's a long story, but yeah, something's up. I'll get through it, though, I mean, *we'll* get through it." It took some getting used to, reminding herself that it was no longer just herself that she needed to worry about.

Miriam squinted at her in the bright sunlight. "Hm. The only thing that man is ever pissed off about is all the ghost drama that comes along with you."

She was good, real good.

"I–"

"Please, please, please don't tell me that you evoked yet another spirit."

Huh. She didn't know what to say. "I'm not entirely sure. Oh hell, yes I am."

"You have got to be kidding me, Naomi."

"I wish I was."

Miriam pinched her face tightly. "Want some advice?"

She nodded weakly.

"Get your head wrapped around this case and leave the drama out of your family life."

If only it were that easy.

SHE WAS FORCING it. Trying too hard. Or maybe it was the depressing, cold rooms filled with the rancid smell of dead animals and decaying feces. It appeared that small rodents and other nameless animals had partied it up in this room and left a mess no one had dared to clean.

Naomi swatted away yet another horsefly. "Okay, can I just say that any photographer that comes in here snapping pictures should have her head examined? This is awful."

"It's all in the name of art." Miriam chuckled. "Are you picking up anything?"

"It's too disgusting to tell." Naomi scrunched up her nose in disgust.

"Stop being a brat. You're here to help me."

Nothing. She couldn't pick up on anything. Maybe it was due to the fact that Lillie was front and center in her thoughts; occupying every inch of space in her mind right now.

"I'm not getting anything. I'm sorry."

"Oh, so that's it? You're just going to give up?" Miriam cursed and glared at Naomi. "Close your eyes, Naomi, and do the thing that you do."

"Is that how you think it works?" Naomi huffed.

If only it were that easy to connect to the spirit world. If it were, she'd be contacting Maggie and Ryan on a daily basis.

She closed her eyes, humoring Miriam.

To her surprise, the air that had been so easy to breathe seconds earlier, became thick and harsh, stealing her breath.

"What's the matter now?" Miriam frowned, but then Naomi saw her brows rise in concern. "Are you okay, Naomi?"

The stairs. The hidden passageway pushed through, and an image of a little girl, dressed in a simple but stained white dress, eyes wide with horror, consumed her brain, blocking all of her senses, forcing her attention on the harrowing sadness in the girl's blue eyes. Lillie.

Naomi could hear Miriam speaking to her, feel her hands on her shoulders, but her words were hazy. The image hit her hard–so distant, yet so familiar. Blonde hair, desperate, blue eyes, a pouting mouth, tiny fists raised in anger, then in terror.

She placed both hands atop her head and wailed. Not accustomed to dealing with the feelings of a child, her brain made an attempt to stop empathizing with the girl for just a moment–all she needed was a second to catch her breath and gain some distance. She used every bit of her strength to block out the sights and sounds of the suffering child.

Lillie. What was she doing reaching out to her here?

"Are you okay?" Miriam held onto her arms and steadied Naomi's wavering legs.

Somehow, she found her words as she saw the menacing frown, the challenge in Lillie's eyes moments before her mind flashed to Holly, sitting in her room with Lillie by her side, the same horrifying gleam in her eyes. Holly. She needed to get to her. But then she remembered that Holly was at school, so this vision… it wasn't taking place in the present.

"Oh my God. Oh my God, Miriam." There was no denying it.

"What? What is it? Did you sense something?"

"It's Holly. She–she's in trouble."

# CHAPTER FOUR

Since Naomi's revelation that Holly was in danger, Miriam hadn't mumbled a word about Naomi blocking out the purpose of their trip to the abandoned building. Not once did she show any signs of annoyance, but as Naomi stood now, facing Bryce, she knew telling Bryce about her recent vision and her old, imaginary friend wouldn't go nearly as well.

"You've got me worried sick, Naomi. Tell me what's going on."

She had called Bryce and asked him to get home as soon as possible. Now, a mere hour later, she felt guilt nagging at her that he had left work so early. But then again, what she had to say was best said now, before she figured out a way to keep Bryce in the dark as she had attempted to so many times before, with her other spirit-driven experiences.

She had promised to be truthful with Bryce about

everything, and the fact that this involved Holly directly made the situation even more urgent.

"Bryce, please keep an open mind and don't be upset with me."

His eyes zeroed in on her, growing wider. "Are you kidding me?" His hand went to his hair, raking away his frustration with her.

She closed her eyes and took a moment to brace herself for the impending argument. "Please. Please listen to me."

"Do I have any other choice?" He paused dramatically. "Do I?"

She ignored his remark and recomposed herself, ready to deliver the news to him that she already knew he had refused to accept and could only hope that he would now listen.

"Can you do me a favor, and let me say what I need to without interrupting me, and then I'll be quiet and let you speak?"

Bryce's eyes narrowed, but he shook his head and remained silent. Good. It was a start.

"I had a vision. While I was working on a case with Miriam."

The words had flown out of her mouth, and she knew she should have omitted that part for later.

"Wait—what?"

She held a finger up to silence him. "Let me continue, and then you can ask me anything you want, yell at me—"

"Don't you do that, Naomi. Don't. This is not normal. What you have going on here, what *we* have going on."

"What happened to not interrupting? Bryce, I don't want to upset you, not for anything, and if I could, I'd keep the whole damn thing to myself." She paused, noting the irritation in his gaze. "But this is important, dammit. This involves your daughter, *our* daughter."

She finally succeeded in silencing him. He was all ears, and she had the floor, so she ran with it. "I am positive that Holly's imaginary friend is most definitely the spirit from my childhood, as I suspected."

"*And?*" His eyes grew wide.

"And…" She cringed, hating to continue.

She watched the shift of his features and waited out the deafening silence that came between them. Would he believe her this time?

He studied her.

He bit down on his lip–hard.

He clenched his fists.

He stepped away from her.

He stepped closer.

Then he walked away.

She knew he needed time to process what she had told him. Anyone would, but she followed him across the room and forced him to look at her–hear what she had to say.

"And I have reason to believe that Lillie is dangerous. She's always been an angry soul, but I felt her…there's more. She wants something from me, and she's using Holly to get to me." She looked up at Bryce's face and then her gaze hit the floor. "I'm sorry." She whispered the words and then watched as he retreated from her sight.

Because she was so deep in thought, she barely heard the sound at first, but then it became impossible not to hear it. A soft giggle came from the other side of the living room. A child's cryptic laughter erupted, but it wasn't Holly, for she was still at school.

"Lillie."

A flash of a face that was somehow both haunting and

innocent came before her. The blonde-haired child couldn't have been more than seven or eight years old, but there was something dark, knowing, powerful, and old as the ages about her eyes that grabbed Naomi. For a split second, she tore her gaze away to see if Bryce was able to see Lillie, but the girl's weeping redirected her attention.

She should have been scared; she should have run.

Instead, a desire to reason with her, to grab this child and protect her came first. "Lillie." Naomi stepped forward slowly and made her way toward Lillie.

Step by step, she kept her focus on the girl, feeling not fear but courage and determination to reach her.

The cries morphed into a piercing howl that hit her ears. Light blinded Naomi, stopping her mid-step. The floor throbbed beneath her feet, walls grew closer. Clasping her ears, Naomi sank to the floor and hummed to herself, trying to block out the raw pain in Lillie's screams.

She dared to look up.

"Naomi! Watch out!" Bryce's voice stopped her short as she turned to see what Lillie had in store for her. A vase flew inches from her head, splattering on the wall behind Naomi, leaving blood-red rose petals and streaming water by her side.

The roses had been a gift from Bryce. He had brought them home last week "just because." Naomi glanced up as Bryce approached.

"What the hell was that?"

"That was Lillie."

He didn't speak, but she wished he had. What she wouldn't give for him to raise his voice in aggravation, for him to pace the floor with irritation marking every step.

How could she make this right? She would give anything

to make this go away.

But she was Naomi. And there was not a hell of a lot she could do about it–about the fact that she took in every emotion of those around her, both living and dead.

At times, it was a gift. At other times, it was a curse.

He would have to deal with it, go through this with her.

Or not, she worried, feeling him pulling away from her. She ached to touch him but didn't dare.

Or not.

THE PAST FEW days, she had found herself at Miriam's door more often than not. Miriam was no closer to solving her case, and although she hadn't come out and said the words, Naomi could feel her friend's disappointment as if it were radiating from her.

"Any new leads?" She probably shouldn't have brought up the case but felt she needed to banish the eight-hundred pound gorilla from the room.

"No." Miriam turned her gaze away from Naomi and studied the floor instead.

"I'm sorry." Naomi reached out and touched Miriam's shoulder. "I wish–"

"No, don't apologize. It's okay, really. I mean, this is just a case, and the other thing you're dealing with affects your life, your family." Miriam's blue eyes misted over as she placed her own hand on Naomi's arm.

Was Miriam getting soft on her? She took that moment to appreciate just how far she and her friend had come from when they had first met. Yes, Miriam was a badass, but she did have a softer side. One only needed to stick around and weed through the sarcasm and pointed digs to get there. But it was worth it.

Maybe it was the rare glimpse of Miriam's softer side. Who knew? But Naomi felt herself give in to her own fragile emotions.

"It's not just a case. A woman was murdered, a woman who had a family, people who loved her." There it was again, that darn empathy sucking her in.

"Oh, no. Don't do that. Please don't." Miriam pulled back, hesitated, but then leaned in and held Naomi close. "Don't cry, honey. It's going to be okay."

How could everything be okay with a troubled ghost-child seeking to make Holly her new "best friend"? This time, it hit way too close to home. In the past, Naomi took solace in the fact that she could shelter Holly, and even Bryce, for the most part, from this tenuous part of her life. She had simply told them to go home, and she alone had dealt with Maggie, Ryan, and then Nick.

This was different. Even Bryce knew it and had failed to communicate what this meant for them and their future together as a family. Over the past few days, Bryce had been cordial but seemed to hold her at a distance. She could hardly blame him.

"I don't want to hurt them, but God, I don't want to lose them either." She was looking to Miriam for answers that she knew her friend didn't have. But at least she could listen.

"What do you think she wants?"

"Oh, hell, who knows? To be my BFF again? To right a wrong? Closure? What do any of them want from me?" Naomi twisted her hands together, her frustration building.

"Don't say that." Miriam's tone came across

uncharacteristically gentle. "You loved Maggie and Ryan."

Of course she did, and she could even admit that she did end up loving her troubled ex-boyfriend Nick a bit in the end. "I know. I still love them, but this girl– Lillie–she's cold and troubled. I feel it, see it. I remember."

"And so was Nick, and you handled him like a champ." Miriam smiled widely, showing off her gorgeous, toothy grin.

So she had.

"I did, didn't I?" She straightened her back. Nick was a challenge, but yes, she had survived.

Barely.

Naomi thought back to her recurring dream but remembered, in her last nightmare, she had survived, and since then, she hadn't experienced the disturbing dream again. Maybe that meant she could deal with anything and cast her fear aside. Maybe it was a message from Nick that she had handled the worst and she would survive this too.

"Yes, kid, you survived, and you will do it again." Miriam stood and turned the coffee pot on. Naomi recalled the endless cups of coffee, sleepless nights, and ensuing arguments with Bryce. They had argued about ghosts, too little sleep, too much coffee…

"I don't want to do this again." Her hands covered her face as her heart sank.

Miriam placed a mug in front of her. "I know, sweetie, but you must, and this time, you need to place equal focus on your family as well."

"Solid advice, but how does one go about helping a malevolent spirit and keeping her marriage strong and her new daughter safe, all at the same time?"

"You're about to find out, and if anyone can do it, my

money's on you." Miriam winked as she poured the fresh, steaming coffee that had served to fuel Naomi through her last battle.

*Here we go.* She lifted the piping hot beverage to her mouth and allowed it to drift deliciously down her belly to warm her insides.

# CHAPTER FIVE

ONE MINUTE SHE was sweet as molasses, the next she was a nightmare. Naomi exercised a profound amount of patience for Holly because she knew Holly was being pulled emotionally from the other side, from Lillie.

"Holly?" Right now, Naomi seemed to have her stepdaughter all to herself. She needed to make the most of this precious time together, just the two of them.

Bryce, powerless to do anything else, had distinctly instructed Naomi not to talk about Lillie, but given the fact that mere moments before, Holly had deliberately stamped down on Naomi's foot, seconds before a book had collided with her head, she figured she'd better act fast.

All Bryce kept repeating was, "*Let me think. Don't make any moves without talking to me.*" The problem was that Bryce wasn't doing anything except ignoring the situation. He had only seen the one time where the vase had smashed to the floor and was trying to justify how it had happened. He hadn't seen Lillie standing there, hadn't witnessed the cascading tears, the howling desperation in her cries. Naomi had gone looking for answers anyway. She had even wandered the secret passageway a few hours earlier, attempting to reconnect with Ellie, or Lillie, or whatever the hell her name was, but to no avail. The darn girl was shutting her out, playing her infamous head games.

"Yes, Naomi?" The title of Mom had disappeared days ago. Now she was simply Naomi. She studied Holly and noted that the circles under her eyes now appeared darker, shadowed.

Couldn't Bryce see that Lillie was not to be ignored? The demanding spirit was starting to take a toll on Holly's attitude, sleep, and from the looks of it, soon it would be her health.

"I believe you." She leaned in, closer, and then closer still, to ensure Bryce didn't hear her from downstairs.

"Huh?"

"I said I believe you. I know your friend Lillie is real."

Holly's eyes grew wide. "You *do?*"

"Yes. Yes, Holly, I do."

Holly moved impossibly close to her. "How? How do you know?" she whispered.

Clutching onto Holly's hands tightly, Naomi knelt as she spoke the words, but forgot to whisper this time. "Because I've seen her. I've seen Lillie, and I've known her–for a very long time as a matter of fact."

"Naomi! That's enough." His firm tone startled her. Bryce stood in the doorway, a scowl lining his face. Holly wasn't the only one with shadows under her eyes. "Holly, you're going to have to excuse Naomi, she tends to get a little carried away with your make believe games." He wouldn't even look at her, wouldn't even cast his eyes in her direction. Would he grow to hate her because of this? The distant thought pounded louder with each passing day.

"No, Daddy, she doesn't."

A storm crossed over Holly's features and Naomi steeled herself for what would come next.

"Yes, Holly. Yes, she does." This was bad. Bryce's gaze hardened.

There was no way she was going to interrupt this power play between father and daughter. All she could do was bounce her attention from one to the other, all the while holding her breath.

"No, Daddy, she doesn't! At least, *she* believes me!"

"It's your imagination, Holly. It's Naomi's as well. She's trying to play with you, but this time she's gone too far, way too far." Bryce's voice finally softened, and Naomi had to give him credit in the patience department. She almost wanted to jump in and agree with him that she did cross the line. Almost.

"I don't like you, either of you, right now!" Turning, Holly's gaze traveled to Naomi, and her mouth set in a firm line. "Mommies are bad sometimes, Naomi, but it's okay because you're not my mommy–my mommy died!" Fury lined her tiny brows and traveled down to her tight fists as her chest heaved.

"Holly!" Bryce reached for Holly, gripping her shoulders. Naomi watched his face contort from anger to sorrow as he tried to deal with his daughter's outburst. All Naomi could do was sit and watch as Holly shook her head while Bryce's face turned a deep crimson shade.

She couldn't sit back and do nothing. The situation

had escalated, and Naomi wasn't one to sit patiently on the sidelines. "Bryce–"

"Not now, not now." He threw his hand back, signaling for her to stay out of it. This was all her fault, how could he possibly expect her to stay out of it? How could he still be in denial after witnessing the vase?

Stepping back, she bit down on her fingertips as she felt the temperature of the room decrease. Bryce and Holly appeared oblivious to the change in temperature, and she could only stand and watch as they continued to bicker back and forth. She couldn't even decipher what they were saying; it was as if she were seeing this play out from a distance. Watching the struggle between two of the people she loved most became too much to bear. The temperature dropped with each second that ticked by.

Now was the time for action.

Since Naomi seemed to be the prime target of Lillie's aggression, she stepped back and inched her way to the door. She could just leave and perhaps lure Lillie so that she would follow her.

But, on second thought, she knew Lillie was smarter than that, and she couldn't leave Bryce and Holly alone. Regardless of how Bryce felt about her role in this mess, Naomi would protect them any way she could.

Bryce kneeled on the floor, talking to Holly, who sat on the bed. Inches over Bryce's head hung a shelf full of knick-knacks. It wobbled, ever so slightly at first, but then the items threatened to spill over. Naomi stepped toward her husband and stepdaughter, reaching out.

"What are you doing?" Bryce's eyes went wide.

There was no time to explain. She pulled at them, but Bryce wouldn't budge. Damn, he wouldn't budge, and

Bryce's head was directly beneath the shelf. She scooped Holly in her arms as Bryce finally moved, seconds before the entire shelf landed on the floor, inches from where he had been.

And then she saw her, the ghostly sheen of the blonde-haired girl, smirking, mocking her. "Lillie. Whatever your problem is, come to me. Leave them alone. You hear?" Naomi could only hope that her thumping heart wouldn't give away her fear.

This time, not only did she and Holly see Lillie, but judging from his expression of shock, Bryce did as well. "Oh my–God," he managed.

Before she had a chance to secure her plan of action, Naomi spun her head as Zelda screeched into the room, hissing wildly. The cat turned her head from Naomi to the spot where Lillie had stood, seconds before. Then Zelda did the strangest thing; she scurried over to the spot where Lillie had been and sat, studying Naomi with a foreign look on her feline face that Naomi couldn't place.

"What is happening here?" Bryce's mouth fell open, and he quickly searched Naomi's face for answers.

"I don't know, Bryce. I don't know, but let me try to figure it out." His eyes gave her the answer she had been waiting for. Now that he was out of the denial stage, she could use his help in trying to figure out the next step. He had helped her before, and she knew they made a pretty good team.

TIME TICKED BY slowly. So slowly, in fact, that Naomi feared she would lose her mind if one more second passed without a word from Bryce. He blamed her for this, of course he blamed her. She blamed herself, and if she could take off, vanish, and bring her troublesome little Lillie with her until she figured this mess out, she would do so in a heartbeat. But she wasn't a fool, and neither was Lillie. Lillie had a purpose, a reason for showing up right now, after all these years, and unfortunately, Holly was closely tied to her plan.

What that purpose was and how deeply Holly was rooted to it was precisely what Naomi needed to figure out. And fast. She suspected Holly was merely a pawn in the larger game of whatever Lillie had in mind, and that didn't sit well with Naomi at all. For a pawn was disposable, and that was not something Naomi could even consider without losing her mind.

Hours ago, Bryce had simply stared at Naomi, scooped a wailing Holly in his arms, and then walked out. She had thought his gut reaction would be to admit his denial and start up one of their brainstorming sessions, complete with coffee and endless notes filled with clues. Unfortunately, he wasn't quite there yet.

Knowing Bryce, he most likely took Holly out for some ice cream, maybe even to the mall. She needed to use this time alone to plan, come up with a course of action.

Something–anything.

When Bryce returned, she would show him that she had a focus for solving this mess. But what could she do? She ran a hand through her hair and twisted the ends.

Once again, Naomi walked the halls, the bedrooms, and then finally the dark stairway that looped itself through the walls, housing secrets that only Lillie was privy to.

"Lillie? Ellie?" Damn, this was a disaster. Naomi wasn't

even sure what name to call this little tyrant of a ghost. Lillie. It was apparently her real name, and that's what she decided she would stick with from this point on. It still baffled Naomi that she had repressed all of the memories of this ghost for so many years. As the floodgates burst open, her mind flooded with stark images of the young girl, her tattered, dirty dress and the false kindness she had used as bait to lure Naomi in, just like she was doing with Holly.

Naomi wondered if her own mother shared the gift, or curse perhaps, of this special sight for unearthly beings. Had Naomi's mom been harassed by Lillie? She couldn't recall any conversations outside of the normal imaginary friend chatter. Her mother had seemed accepting, if not entertained by the notion of an imaginary friend. She couldn't exactly ask her mom, as her parents had passed years ago. Her parents had been much older when they had Naomi, and she considered them lucky to lead the full lives they had lived until their deaths, one after the other it had seemed. Naomi figured their love had been special, so intense that her father simply couldn't bear to be in this world without her mom, and that his heart had failed to beat without her love. She had heard of this phenomenon so many times before and believed it fully, believed in true love.

"Where are you, you little troublemaker?" Naomi called out into the darkness.

A faint snicker.

Okay, so that was the way to evoke this spirit. "Huh. You heard that, didn't you? Well, it's true. You're a brat and a spoiled one at that."

Silence. Something ticked at Naomi, telling her she may have gone too far with that comment.

Before she had a chance to consider the fact further, she

felt a sudden push. Stumbling backward, she placed her hands beneath her, finding her way to standing position, only to be knocked down once more.

Was it safer to stay put or risk getting pushed down again? "Lillie? I'm sorry, but the truth is the truth. If you have a problem, come to me. Leave Holly out of it. She's just as child. You should know better."

No response. Well, that could be a good thing, or it could be a bad thing. Naomi took a chance and stood up, catching her breath.

Turns out it was the latter. She lost her footing and felt a strong force push her harder. With no railing to hold onto, Naomi gripped the bare wall with her hands and cried out. Sweat laced her forehead as she clenched her muscles tighter against the impossible force. Her feet came out from under her, and she stumbled recklessly down the dirt stained stairway, hands flailing, reaching out for the walls. She cried out, twisting her foot beneath her and smacking her chin on the bottom landing.

Damn. That hurt.

"I was just a child, too. It would serve you well to remember that. Consider this your first lesson." Lillie's voice took on a mature tone, not unlike that of an old schoolteacher. A smug giggle followed up on the comment.

First lesson? The child's words were a clue, they had to be.

Fighting back tears, Naomi clutched her ankle, trying to bite past the excruciating pain. "Lillie…" She needed to keep this conversation going.

But just like that, the little blonde terror disappeared, leaving Naomi with a world of questions.

# CHAPTER SIX

"Wʜᴀᴛ ᴛʜᴇ ʜᴇʟʟ is going on here?"

Wonderful. Bryce had returned with Holly, spying her lying at the bottom of the stairs. Next time, she needed to remember to push the stove in the kitchen back just enough so that Bryce wouldn't catch her navigating behind the walls of the kitchen.

"Oh my God–are you okay?" Now that he saw she was hurt, his features softened in time with his tone. Bryce told Holly to run upstairs and get into her pajamas.

"You shouldn't mess with Lillie," Holly whispered before turning to follow Bryce's directions.

Both she and Bryce gaped at Holly's retreating form as she made her way to her bedroom. Right now, she needed to get out of this dusty space and get some ice on her ankle, not to mention her chin.

"Help me up." She reached her hand out to Bryce, and

he gently guided her into his arms.

"Naomi. I'm sorry. I'm so sorry about this. I shouldn't have left you." He smoothed her hair back, searching her face for forgiveness. "I'm sorry." He placed kisses over her chin and up the length of her face.

"Don't be. I've been nothing but a huge pain in the ass, but let's save that conversation for later. I need to sit and get some ice on my ankle."

Gingerly, Bryce placed her on the couch and bent down to take a look at her swollen ankle and then gently cupped her chin in his hands. "I think I need to get you to a doctor, Naomi." He ran his thumb over her aching skin.

"Ouch." She winced and swatted his hand to the side. She knew he was only trying to help. "Let's see how I look in the morning. Can you grab me some ice and ibuprofen?" That should at least get her through the night.

"Of course." Bryce returned moments later with an ice pack, a glass of water, and two pills. "Naomi. I have to ask, what were you doing in there?" His tone grew anxious. Of course he knew who she had been looking for.

Naomi had shared her first adventure within the walls with Bryce days earlier, and he had requested that she not return to the spot. Besides being haunted with spirits, Naomi knew Bryce was worried that the space wasn't up to code and presented safety concerns. Well, turns out he was right, but the fact was that Lillie could appear anywhere in this house if she pleased.

"I don't want to argue about this right now."

"Nobody's arguing, but I thought we had discussed this."

Naomi sighed deeply. "I wanted to fix this, and I went looking directly for the source."

He nodded his head and looked away. True to his word,

he didn't argue, but the silence was worse. How many times would she continue to disappoint him?

As if reading her mind, Bryce locked eyes with her and spoke, "I might not love what's happening here or what you brought into this house with you, but dammit, Naomi, I love you and don't want to see you hurt. I just feel so–helpless."

Relief spread through her veins, and she cried out, "I love you, too." She reached for him and held him tightly, wishing that they only had regular, minor troubles to bicker over, like forgetting to pick up milk at the grocery store.

"Bryce. I don't know what she wants. She won't tell me. I don't know what to do."

"I see that. And once again, I'm beyond helpless, and it's killing me, Naomi, killing me."

"I know."

"And this time, both you and Holly are directly affected, and I'd rather die than to see any harm come to either of you."

She fought off the chilling possibility that he actually could die if she didn't stop this madness. She had thought it before, but now she had to put a voice to her thoughts. She had to. "I could leave, just for a little while."

His eyes held hers, and the pain was raw. "What are you talking about?"

"I could see if Miriam wants some company for a while, just to put some space between me and you guys. Maybe Lillie would seek me out over there, away from Holly."

"And maybe she wouldn't. She's *here,* Naomi, *here.*"

"I get that, but she's using Holly to get to me. I feel it."

"Then following that logic, she's going to continue to use her and pull you back here." It was true she supposed. He lifted his head and spoke again. "Why now, Naomi? Why?

That's what I can't figure out."

She had wondered just the same thing. Why had Lillie disappeared for all these years? Why hadn't she shown up when Naomi lived up the road all alone?

"I have no clue. Maybe it's this house?"

"This house. Okay then, if you leave, it will be me and Holly battling this girl alone, and I have to admit that I'm out of my realm of experience with ghosts. Doesn't leave me feeling very manly, now that I think about it." He scratched at the stubble growing on his chin.

He had almost chuckled with the admission. When was the last time they had laughed together? Really laughed? Not since Lillie had shown her face, that was for sure.

"Um–I kind of have to agree with you on that one, but you are a man–pure man." He pulled her close, and she snuggled into his shoulder, inhaling his familiar, clean, most definitely male scent.

"You're not going anywhere, you hear?"

"Okay." She closed her eyes, not sure if she could trust herself to keep her word, but for now, she would just enjoy the feeling of peace.

"So what's on the agenda for today?"

Miriam glared at Naomi as she sipped at her coffee. Naomi almost laughed aloud. She recalled a time when Miriam had lectured her, along with Bryce, of course, about her caffeine habit. Seemed Miriam had a habit of her own to conquer, Naomi knew that now wasn't the time to bring it up.

"We go back to the scene of the crime, and *this* time, you pay attention and focus on the job, not your child ghost." Her lack of patience on the case and for Naomi's ghost issues had returned with a vengeance.

"Yes, ma'am." She threw her hand up in salute as she watched Miriam closely. Her brows were tightly drawn, and a scowl lined her otherwise gorgeous face. The stress had started to take a toll on her.

"Everything okay?" She studied her friend.

"Yes, no. Oh, hell. It's this damn case. I can't get any solid leads, and it's just not acceptable."

Ah, the perfectionist. She wondered if there was ever a case that Miriam had failed to crack. Again, not the right time to ask.

"I see. I'll try really hard this time."

A smile lightened Miriam's features. "You will? For real?"

"For real." Time away from her problems at hand could only be a good thing. She would certainly give it her best effort.

"Let's hit the road. You can bring your coffee in one of those cups if you want."

Miriam nodded her head toward a stack of disposable cups tucked into a corner of the counter as Naomi gulped back her remaining coffee. "I'm good. Let's go."

Neither said a word as they headed out the door into the brisk, late autumn air. The air held memories of the past. It had also been autumn when her tiny, safe world imploded tenfold with the appearance of Maggie, her treasured friend. Even though she had never known Maggie in life, she still considered the spirit a friend and always would. Funny how the simplest shift in temperature, the vivid red of the leaves, and the swirl of the crisp wind around her brought Maggie and Ryan crashing back to her.

"What's on your mind?"

Her melancholy mood broke as she was brought back to the present. "Just my wandering mind, nothing for you to worry about."

"Hm." Miriam cast a sideways look at Naomi as she pulled out onto the street beyond. "That seems to happen a lot, that wandering mind of yours."

What could she say? Miriam was right, of course. Seems that Miriam was right about a lot of things. She was a good person, a solid friend. Naomi only wished that Miriam would get the life she deserved, complete with a man who was lucky enough to deserve her. Little Miss Tough As Nails would make a wonderful wife and mother one day, for the loyalty and love she showered on those she chose to be close with was fierce and unbending.

"*Now* what are you thinking about?" Miriam kept her eyes on the road, a smirk in place on her beautiful face.

"You don't want to know, trust me." A giggle escaped Naomi's lips as she took in Miriam's profile. Besides her successful career and strong personality, with those high cheekbones, striking blue eyes, and porcelain smooth skin, Miriam was most definitely a catch. The only problem was matching Miriam with someone deserving and strong enough to keep up with her.

Resting her head on the seat, Naomi's mind shifted back to the case at hand. "So there's nothing new at all with the case?"

"Nope, like I said, the whole situation is unnervingly quiet. Oh, but the woman's brother called me several times, and he's meeting up with me after we're finished at the scene and I drop you off."

"Oh, okay. Want me to come along?"

Miriam hesitated but only for a split second. "Sure." Did Miriam wish to only include Naomi in certain parts of the investigation?

"Listen, if you'd rather—"

"No, you should come. I need your help, and whatever input you can offer can only help, right?"

"Right." Naomi tilted her head, gazing out at the colorful play of leaves decorating the trees. "This brother, was he close to the victim?"

"Yes, Cole claims he and Sharon were quite close, being the only children of a tight knit family growing up. They were only two years apart. He says he disliked Sharon's husband pretty much from the start."

"Didn't you say there was nothing new to report?" Miriam should know that any piece of information could be a possible clue.

"I guess I forgot to tell you, but you're right, I should have. The ex-husband stinks from a mile away as far as I'm concerned, alibi or not."

Naomi didn't necessarily think, just because the victim's brother disliked the ex, that it made him a viable suspect, but she kept her opinion to herself. She knew the cliché that it was always the husband sometimes rang true, but in her mind, that excluded other possible suspects. For now, she would consider the possibility but leave it as just that, a possibility.

Once they arrived at the old facility, they headed straight inside. Naomi could swear that there was a shift in the air around her. She closed her light jacket tightly around her. "Do you feel that?"

Miriam's jaw set tight as she ignored Naomi's comment.

She went about searching the floor, touching the spray-painted, stained, dark walls. Naomi followed suit and reached out her own hand, looking for a tactile connection—she placed her other hand out and traced the rough edges of the wall—bleak and cold. There was something different here, something that wasn't here last time, but Naomi couldn't quite place it. There-there it was, clearly scripted on the far side of the room. Her own name had been spray-painted on the walls in a bright, vibrant red. The handwriting immature, scratchy. Before her, each of the four walls surrounding them were covered by her name, only her name. Hundreds upon hundreds of times, Naomi saw her own name, each one in a dripping red immature print.

Before she had time to see Miriam's reaction, she heard her name being called.

*Naomi.*

She snapped her head around to face Miriam. "Did you hear that?"

"What?"

"The—my name. Someone called my name."

Miriam shook her blonde mane and narrowed her eyes. "Um, no. Can't say that I did." With that, Miriam spun her head back to the walls where Naomi's name had adorned nearly every square inch seconds before. Now, the walls were devoid of her name, appearing the same as they had the first time she had visited the building days ago.

"Did you—?"

But Miriam didn't hear her, she was in her intense focus mode, her eyes taking in the surfaces, which held nothing unusual.

Steeling herself against the wall, Naomi's heart rate slowed down as she told herself she had merely imagined the writing, the soft voice that had called out to her moments before. Soft and familiar, the voice had been distant but so familiar.

It was her.

Lillie.

She knew it like she knew the back of her hand. "She's here."

"She–who?"

Shaking her head, Naomi knew there was a reason for the spirit being in this location, but right now, she couldn't figure it out.

"The girl, the spirit from my house." Naomi had given Miriam the short version of the little girl who had haunted her thoughts since childhood; now she filled in the gaps as she watched Miriam's face transform from disbelief to horror.

"Here? She's right *here?*" Miriam snapped her head around, scanning the room.

"Don't worry. She's not here to bother you. It's me she wants. Isn't that right, Lillie?" Naomi threw her arms out wide, shouting the words. Her grand gesture earned a cryptic chuckle from the other side of this world.

"Shit, Naomi. Shit."

"Yup, I'm in a world of it, too, thanks to this little charmer."

Another chuckle, this time a bit darker.

"She doesn't sound very charming to me." Miriam leaned closer to Naomi and whispered, "How old is she?"

"Eh, most likely seven? Eight?"

Clutching her chest, Miriam pulled Naomi closer. The rare sight of Miriam displaying any type of weakness startled Naomi.

"Are you okay?" She placed a gentle hand on Miriam's

back and leaned down to swipe the hair from her friend's face.

"Just give me a minute. You and your ghosts, you're killing me, Naomi."

Was she actually afraid of something? Ghosts? "Are you afraid of them?" She tried not to allow her shock to show as she spoke the words.

"Damn. Yes, and you can keep your snide remarks to yourself. When all this started with Maggie and Ryan, I could almost handle it. But Nick? He threw me over the edge, that one."

Understandable, and the fact that Phil had been so deeply involved certainly didn't help matters. Phil had been responsible for Nick's death. His reach was long, Phil had gotten to him from within the inside of the prison walls and had used Miriam to execute his plan. Naomi still couldn't believe Miriam had dated Phil, but she supposed the fact that he was Ryan's brother made him seem trustworthy. But Naomi hadn't liked Phil, practically from the start. He was everything Ryan wasn't—cruel, twisted, and disturbed.

Naomi took hold of Miriam's hand as she sighed and looked around.

"I can see how that could have happened. Hell, I'm shocked you bought my house, what with the history and all."

"Yeah, well. You know how much I love that house, and I figured your magnetism would pull any spirits right to you."

"You weren't wrong there. Now for this little troublemaker."

"Naomi, she's a kid, this Lillie, she's just a child."

That was the tough part. "I realize that, but she's had over a century to hone her skills at making people's lives miserable." Her tone increased as she spoke the last words.

"Go easy, here. Be gentle with her."

Of course, Naomi couldn't forget the fact that, however horrifying the spirit was, it still belonged to what was once an innocent child. As much as she wished the little girl would just disappear from their lives, recently she had been thinking more and more of how she could reach her. She was sure she could help Lillie, if only the child would allow her to do so.

Zelda popped into her thoughts, more specifically the image of her running to the spot where Lillie had stood and the strange look on her face. There was something to that swift action on her cat's part, but now wasn't the time to ponder over it, now she needed to help Miriam.

"Sorry about all of this. It seems each time we come here, I make this more and more about my own problems."

"True," Miriam agreed. "True, but not your fault."

Naomi tried to clear all thoughts of Lillie and Zelda from her mind as she made her way around the room. Something was off here. She felt nothing; nothing amiss about the crime, nothing in this room. She glanced upward, toward the ceiling, as a flash burst through of a woman and a man.

"We're in the wrong room." She felt it with certainty. "She may have been found in this room, but she didn't die here, didn't struggle with the murderer here."

"But her body was found here. How do you know that?" Miriam's eyes held Naomi's as she clasped her hands.

"I–"

"Forget it, I don't want to know. Lead the way." She stepped back, allowing Naomi to take a path toward the stairwell.

Images of a struggle, loud, shouting voices filled the

space in Naomi's head as she shuddered, attempting to block out the negative vibes threatening to envelop her.

*A man's hand–pulling at her, grabbing at her hair, dragging the frightened woman up the stairs. She could see the gloved male hand, but not the man's face. She heard shouting, a man's shouts mixed with the woman's cries.*

*"Mine. You're mine!"*

*"You're hurting me!"*

*"Cheating piece of–"*

*"Stop!"*

This room.

"Here." She practically choked on the thick emotion she had sucked in. Taking a few steady breaths, Naomi allowed herself a moment to compose herself as she fought back the rising tears.

"Are you okay?" Miriam's hand touched hers, and the comfort of a friend was exactly what Naomi needed to pull through the last vision.

She pressed her eyes shut tight, freeing up her thoughts to finish what she had started here. The pounding in her head returned as she witnessed the final breath escape from the woman, watching her eyes as strong hands reached up, lifting the woman off the ground. Her struggle was futile; any attempts at grasping for the man's hands were met with fury.

*"Mine, mine, mine. Now you're all mine."*

The worst part of all was standing back, witnessing the fear in the woman's eyes, knowing she could do nothing to help her. How alone and terrified she must have been in those last moments.

Sick, maniacal bursts of shouting, then a twisted laughter, melding with the softer giggles of a young girl. Laughter from the man increased as the wails of Lillie took over. Her laughter now shifted to a howling sadness, which shockingly now matched the cries of the man who had murdered Sandra.

"Stop it, stop!" Naomi witnessed the gloved hands carrying the body down the stairs to a more cluttered room; one that he must have thought easier to attempt to hide the body.

Naomi fell to the floor, sobbing openly, not feeling anything but the deep, internal fatigue these souls placed inside of her. She vaguely registered Miriam's hands pressing down on her, rubbing her back.

She opened her eyes, her gaze stuck on the far wall across the room. The place where the man had taken the life of Sharon Wilde.

Were the cries even real, or had Lillie simply interjected, wishing to screw with Naomi, confuse her?

But it had all seemed so real. Was he sorry for what he had done? Did he realize his mistake too late? Or was he just mourning his own sorry self?

"Over there." Naomi gestured toward the old crumbling fireplace. "But he was wearing black gloves, heavy black gloves." Naomi wrapped her hands around her head and waited for the shaking to stop.

"Here?" Miriam stood, equipped with her camera and plastic bag. She lifted her camera, snapping picture after picture and then scooped up the items surrounding the crime scene. With a sigh, she called in to the station. Naomi knew what her friend must be thinking. Miriam's partner would be pissed that she had yet again investigated during her own time. Miriam had shared that when it came to working with Naomi, she felt it best it was only the two of them without the distraction of a person who didn't understand Naomi's capabilities.

Facts piled through Naomi's thoughts, the words the man had spoken. It had to be the ex-husband. It had to be. But with a solid alibi, how could they prove it? The possibility the killer had been a hit man entered Naomi's mind briefly, but she squashed it just as quickly. The emotion–jealousy, possessiveness–it came from someone who had once been very close with the woman.

Miriam returned to her side, impatience etched her features. "What else? What did you see? Tell me everything."

"He knew her. He knew her very well. He told her she was a cheater. *Mine, you're all mine.*" He kept repeating the words."

"The ex, but how could that be?" She could see the wheels turning, knew that Miriam, too, was fixated on disputing the alibi.

"Seems that it's him, but I can't be sure." What she didn't tell Miriam was Lillie's part in the unveiling of the crime. She didn't possess the energy right now, and she supposed it wasn't relevant to the case.

Miriam swiped her cell phone from her pocket and activated the keyboard, jabbing her finger over the screen. "Is this what he looked like?"

A photo of a man in his mid-thirties was thrust in front of her. Her head continued to pound fiercely. "I don't know."

"What? How could you not know?" Miriam barked out. She didn't attempt to mask her impatience. This was the Miriam she had first met and disliked, but now she simply knew that this was the Miriam who got business done. This was the Miriam who grasped at clues, relentless to solve her crimes.

"I didn't see him. I only saw his hands."

"Shit, Naomi. Shit." Miriam turned away and paced silently until Naomi heard the slam of a car door and the sound of footsteps approaching from below.

# CHAPTER SEVEN

Zelda. No, it wasn't Naomi's imagination, that cat was behaving strangely. That is, stranger than usual. Since arriving back home, she wondered how long Zelda had been walking around stealthily, eyes scanning around the room, howling? Problem was, this behavior wasn't completely out of the ordinary. Her cat had been particularly close with the spirit of Maggie and seemed to have a sixth sense for picking up on paranormal activity.

"What's going on, girl?"

Zelda responded with an emphatic meow. "Hm." Naomi bent down and then scooped her cat into her arms. She placed a quick kiss on top of the cat's head, murmuring to Zelda. The cat didn't have any answers, of course, but she did promise herself to pay a bit more attention to Zelda's actions.

"Hey you," Bryce mumbled as he approached her from behind, placing a kiss on the back of her head.

"Hey." She released Zelda and turned to face Bryce. He planted a soft kiss on her lips then traced the outline of her mouth with a gentle finger. "You'd better be careful there. Holly will see us."

"Holly's at her friend's house." His tone grew softer as he kissed her mouth once more, this time with a touch of impatience. "Come closer." He pulled her so near that she could almost match the beat of his heart pounding with hers. She knew this was Bryce's way of dealing with their stress, his way of showing her that he was still there for her.

"Bryce."

"Shh. You talk too much." He pulled her hand and led her to the fireplace. The vision of the crumbling fireplace from the facility threatened to break the mood, but Naomi bit down on her lip and focused her energy on the amazing man before her.

A child's voice boomed across the room. "You love him. Don't you? Be careful to protect the things you love. You never know when he could turn on you and betray you forever. Consider that your next lesson, lesson number two."

What the hell was Lillie spouting off about? She blocked out Lillie, the murder in the old hospital, and all of her worries as she gave in to Bryce's demanding kisses. Lillie persisted, but Naomi ignored her incessant whining. Seems she didn't enjoy being ignored.

Bryce stiffened slightly, breaking their embrace. "Did you hear that?" Worry creased his brows.

She chuckled slightly and turned his face toward her. "Shut up. You talk too much." And then he was hers, all hers, as she guided him down to the rug and placed soft kisses over his face and neck. He grit out her name, reaching for her hand, he entwined it in his. Bryce filled her senses, leaving her wanting more until she practically begged for him to touch her.

"Bryce."

"Shh." He silenced her, molding his body against hers as he whispered her name again and again. She closed her eyes, holding tightly to this very moment, wanting it to never end.

Fear crept its way into the darkest corner of her mind, breaking her concentration as she attempted to forget what Lillie had just said about betrayal. Bryce would never betray her…he loved her too much. Why had Lillie said that?

"I love you." Naomi breathed the words into his ear, and then kissed him with all of her being. She would not let the words come between them.

"I love you, too."

*For now.*

The words popped into her head and, as much as she knew it was a trick of the mind, a small part of the warning stayed with her, tiny enough to give life to the worry that she and Bryce may not make it through this unscathed. Flashes of her struggles with Nick, and similar mind games, pulsed through her mind, and as much as she tried to squash the harsh images, they persisted. Closing her eyes, she felt the warmth of tears slip from her eyes.

THIS TIME IT wasn't Nick she dreamt of, but Lillie. It seemed the little girl had successfully ended her lingering Nickmares, as she had come to term them, and instead replaced them with her own twist on torturing her throughout the night. It figured. The child was egocentric, even in the midnight hours.

Once upon a time, in her dream, Lillie had once been a beautiful blonde haired girl with a delightful, sunny disposition. Naomi followed the vision of her lucid dream. She watched as Lillie's bright blue eyes sparkled, hugging a woman. It had to be her mother. Daughter and mother pounded dough, sprinkled flour, as they baked a pie together, dressed in plain, long white dresses.

"Mother?" Lillie pulled at her apron, her brows creased.

"Don't fuss so, Lillian. Keep your apron on."

"It makes me feel warm, Mother."

"You can take it off soon, we're almost finished. Your father will love the pie, and I know he will be pleased that you've helped out."

"Yes, Mother. Could I play afterward?"

"Yes, dear. Will you go see if Suzanne can play with you?"

Lillie scrunched up her face. "I don't like playing with her. She's bossy. Besides, I want to explore."

"We've talked about this, Lillian. It's not healthy for you to spend so much time alone."

Lillie hung her head and mumbled something incoherent. Her mother snatched her hand and reprimanded her. "That is not respectful behavior. Now, speak to me properly. Look me in the eye, and say your words clearly. You hear?"

"Yes, Mother."

"Now, you'll go and knock on Suzanne's door, and use your manners."

"Yes, Mother."

Her mother smiled sweetly and bent to kiss her daughter's head. "That's my girl. And remember, I don't want you poking around the stove again."

Lillie turned her head toward the stove, fixing her gaze on

the area near the floor. "I thought I heard someone. I really think I did."

With a loud sigh, her mother removed Lillie's apron and placed her hands on her own hips. "Or something more like it. I told you we have mice, dear, and mice are filled with disease. I don't want you going back there again, ever. Am I clear? We wouldn't want your father to find out you've disobeyed."

"Yes, ma'am." Had there been harsh consequences for disobeying? Were these the lessons Lillie spoke of?

"Excuse me?" Lillie's mother lifted her daughter's chin with her hand until their eyes met.

"Yes, ma'am." Lillie enunciated louder this time.

"Very well, then, off you go." The woman turned back to attend to her baking as Lillie remained still, her eyes on her mother.

"Mother?"

"Yes, what is it?"

"I love you, and I'm sorry."

Naomi could tell that Lillie didn't like to disappoint her mother; didn't like to learn her "lessons."

"I love you, too, now. Just remember our talk, you understand?"

Lillie nodded, over and over, but her eyes fixed to a point near the back of the stove.

Although her vision centered mostly on Lillie, something nagged Naomi about the unfocused image of Lillie's mother in the background. Was it thoughts of lessons? No, there was something else, but she couldn't put her finger on it.

Lillie wouldn't listen, she would go back there, probably many times. What did this all mean? Was it just random streams of consciousness? Naomi became aware of that fact that although her dream wasn't real, it instilled a source of terror within her, the sweet scene of mother and daughter baking together was a prelude to the horror that would surely follow. She slowly drifted in and out of consciousness as the murky fog started to lift.

Naomi breathed deeply, gasping at the foreign feeling of someone tugging at her. She woke, facing a pair of angry, cornflower blue eyes bearing down on her.

"Lesson number three: don't trust anyone, especially those who claim to love you. They all lie, and they all hurt you." It wasn't over, not yet. "And lesson number four: be sneaky, be smart, and learn to lie so you won't get caught."

She needed to be smart and calm here, any show of fear on her part would fuel Lillie's fire. "Lillie. What happened to you? Did you go back to the spot near the stove? What did you find? What did you see there?" She realized the questions were being fired faster than the girl could answer, but her mind couldn't slow down.

"Nobody cares about me. What difference does it make?" Venom spewed from her eyes as she clenched her tiny fists. Naomi felt Lillie's powerful weight holding her down, even though the girl's hands didn't touch her body. She had the ability to use the sheer power of her mind to manipulate objects and people around her. It was worse than she had thought.

From the distance, Naomi could hear Zelda approaching, howling her distress. This might not be the safest place for her cat. She silently willed Zelda to stay put but knew how relentless Zelda could be.

"I care."

"Liar, liar, pants on fire." Lillie showed her inner child by crossing her arms and pouting.

"I do. I want to help you. Who wronged you? I can help

if you just trust me." As soon as the words left her mouth, she realized her mistake. Trust. Obviously Lillie had trust issues. Damn, what was wrong with her?

"Trust? You speak of trust?" Lillie's words thundered around her, shook the walls of the room. Zelda screeched, drawing closer. Too much was transpiring here in too short of a span. Naomi needed to get control of the situation and fast.

Without thinking through the consequences of her actions, Naomi did what she did best–gave a piece of herself. She wrapped her arms around the small child, feeling the frigid temperature of Lillie's skin, attempting to warm her.

Cold–she was so, so cold. Naomi's heart broke for the girl as her soul attempted to make contact with Lillie's. No surprise that Lillie blocked her, keeping Naomi and her empathy at arm's length. A gripping fear strangled her empathy for the child, and she knew that Lillie felt it. One look into the fury on Lillie's face and she regretted her actions. She shouldn't have embraced her so impulsively.

Lillie stole her breath as Naomi felt the sheer power of the girl's rage. Just as Zelda sprinted into the room, she felt her body lift up from the bed. Powerless to stop the events quickly unfolding, all she could do was close her eyes and beg. Lillie kept her suspended, hovering mid-air until with the flick of Lillie's wrist and a cold glare in her eyes, Lillie slammed her into the wall.

"Lesson number five: don't ever lay your hands on me again. Ever. I'm stronger than you, stronger than you can even imagine." Naomi didn't dare interrupt. "You see, the two people I loved most in my life used to hug me, tell me they loved me…"

Torn between wanting to protect Zelda and needing to

hear more about Lillie's past, Naomi held her breath and kept her eyes steeled on her cat. *Don't move.* She silently pleaded with Zelda to be still.

"A mother and a father. Can you imagine that?"

Imagine what, Lillie? Imagine what? Her mind spoke the question her voice could not. She didn't move for fear she would break the spell of Lillie's confessions.

"My own parents betrayed me, they sealed my fate, led me to where I stand now."

Tears streamed openly down Lillie's face as she listened to the precocious words spewing from Lillie's mouth.

"Parents whom I once loved, parents whom I trusted, my mother, my father, they did this. *They did this to me!*" She shrieked the last words, dropping her hands and sliding to the floor. Naomi lifted her hand but then recalled the girl's strict command to never touch her. Her heart swelled for this little girl who had been through God only knows what. She couldn't even imagine what had turned that sweet girl from her dream into this venomous, vengeful spirit.

Finally, Naomi found her voice. "Lillie." Her voice shook with raw emotion. "I saw you–in my dreams. You were amazing. Sweet, loving–"

Lillie stopped Naomi with a slam of her hands on the floor. "What I was and who I used to be have no importance to what I am now."

"That's not true."

"Unfortunately, it is, and it's certainly none of your business. You have a role to play here, just like Bryce and Holly." A snicker followed the statement, and Naomi realized that of all the things this spirit had ever stated, her last words were by far the most frightening of all.

"Talk to me. Tell me what you want, what you need."

This was pointless she knew, but what else could she do? She had to try, had to keep Lillie talking.

"What I *want*. What I *need* is for you to hurt just as much as I have, for someone to feel an ounce of my pain. "

"Why Lillie? What will that help? It can't erase the past."

"Shut up. Why should *you* get to be happy when I couldn't? Holly would be better off without you in her life."

A shiver coursed through her body as she considered the implications of Lillie's words. How far would she go to secure this belief?

"Don't say that. That's not true. I love Holly."

"Bull. Bullshit, bullshit, bullshit. Mothers lie, so that makes you a liar by default." Laughter erupted as Naomi closed her eyes, trying to gather her strength. "Even though you're not a *real* mother, not yet." More laughter. A pointed look in the direction of Naomi's belly confirmed her suspicion that Lillie knew way too much about her personal life. She and Bryce had recently tried to start having a baby, but with the appearance of Lillie, Naomi knew the time wasn't right. She wouldn't put her baby in danger. Once this whole mess was sorted out, she would try again.

"Have you told him?"

"Don't."

"Ah. So you haven't. You and I both know how much Bryce wants another child."

"Then leave us alone."

"If you don't tell him, I will."

Damn. "He would understand, given the circumstances." At least she hoped he would. How long could this nonsense go on for?

"I wouldn't be so sure of that, Naomi. You see, I notice a lot of things around here. Like the way his gaze lingers after you've walked out of a room. And not the way it used to, not in a good way."

Before she had a chance to make sense of Lillie's offbeat comment, Naomi noticed Zelda pausing to stare up at Lillie. Her eyes appeared bright and hopeful.

Two things became evident at once. First, she realized that out of most of the spirits she had known, Lillie had the ability to communicate the most clearly and effectively. Was it the fact that she was a child? Did any innocence that may have clung to her give her the power to speak so effectively without the barrier of becoming jaded by everyday life? She thought of Ryan then and considered that, he, too, could communicate with her, but not the whole truth, as he had been in denial of his own death at the time. With Lillie, it was different–the spirits had all seemed so different from one another, but similar in the way that they each needed something from her.

And the other thing? Zelda.

At the sight of her cat, Lillie's eyes popped open wide, and the most precious smile consumed her small face. "Duchess. Duchess, I knew you'd remember me!" At that, Zelda sprung up, landing squarely in Lillie's arms.

Her mind tried to grasp hold of what this might mean. First, Zelda clearly appeared to like this little tyrant. And *Duchess?*

"Um–her name isn't Duchess, that's Zelda." Naomi could hear the deep purrs of satisfaction and affection from Zelda as Lillie stroked her fur.

"You're wrong." Lillie was again back to acting exactly like the child she was, sticking her tongue out at Naomi. "Her name is most certainly Duchess."

# CHAPTER EIGHT

"WE NEED TO talk, Bryce."

He gazed out the window watching Holly play hopscotch in the driveway. Naomi peeked her head over his shoulder and winced as Holly spoke to what appeared to be thin air. From the look of things, the conversation seemed to be going well. She and Lillie must be taking turns, Naomi mused, as she spied Holly waiting out minutes at a time before returning to her turn on the board.

"Jesus, Naomi." Bryce winced as Zelda rubbed up against nothing, meowing upward. She could swear that if cats had the ability to grin, that's precisely what Zelda was doing, and she knew exactly who captured the cat's attention. Or was it Duchess who rubbed against Lillie right now? What could the name Duchess even mean? The bizarre scene unfolding outdoors stole her attention. She couldn't think about the name thing right now.

A random thought popped into Naomi's head and she shared it without thinking. "Well, at least Miriam is our only neighbor, or else people would think we're all crazy." She imagined what the scene outside would look like to a passerby.

At that, Bryce turned to face her. "I really don't care what the hell anyone thinks about us. What I care about is keeping my family safe, and right now, that involves me going outside to break up this little game of ghoulish hopscotch."

Ouch.

She really needed a moment alone with him, but he turned away from Naomi and shook his head. She watched him make his way to the front door, cursing under his breath. He hated her. No, she knew he actually didn't, but at this precise moment, he acted as if he did. Was this what Lillie had been referring to? The looks she couldn't catch as she walked away from him? They did need to talk, and she knew it had to be soon, before Lillie spilled the beans and made things more tenuous than they already were.

"Bryce—"

"Not now, not now." He opened the front door and sprinted to the driveway, calling out Holly's name. What could she do? The only thing that came to mind was to be honest with him about waiting for a better time to have a baby. She figured he would agree with her anyway. Biting down on her fingernail, she viewed Bryce throwing his hands in the air at a, well, for lack of a better word, pissed looking Holly. Zelda continued her dance of rubbing against Lillie, whom she could now clearly see with her own eyes. Zelda appeared to actually love this girl. If only she could speak, what would the cat tell her?

Then they were back. "I want to play with her, Daddy.

She says you're mean and want to spoil all the fun. She says you only pretend to care about me, that you want to send me away so you and Mommy can be all alone. Is it true? Are the two of you going to send me away?" Her face scrunched with worry.

"Holly, Holly, is that what you think?" Bryce kneeled down so that he could make direct eye contact with Holly. He gently turned her so that she faced him. Naomi watched the scene unfold as she twirled the ends of her hair and bit down on her lip. This was bad. Real bad. That little manipulator was doing some serious damage. Naomi needed to pay attention to everything Lillie said and did, no matter how trivial. After nothing but years to stew over her problems and plans for exacting some kind of revenge, every word, every action on Lillie's part had to mean something, must be related to her turmoil.

"Yes, and I agree with her. Naomi is probably an evil woman, just like Lillie says. She came into our lives to take you away from me."

It took every bit of reserve to hold back and let Bryce handle the situation. She ran her hand through her hair, twisting, pulling, turning,

"Honey, Naomi is the least evil person I know, besides you, that is. Trust me. She loves you like you are her own daughter."

Holly paused, lifting her gaze and locking eyes on Naomi, a smirk set on her face. "She doesn't have her own daughter. Lillie told me a secret today."

Naomi gasped as her stomach dropped. No. She wouldn't. Of course she would. That little terror of a ghost would do what she could to wreak havoc around this house, and she knew precisely which buttons to push.

"Holly—"

"Shush, Lillie wants me to tell, and right now, I like Lillie a lot more than I like you."

"Holly!" Bryce's gaze drifted to Naomi. All she could do was watch this play out unless she said the words first, that is.

"Bryce. Let's wait to have a baby, wait until we figure this Lillie thing out."

"What?" His mouth fell as an incredulous look came over his face. "Now isn't the time to discuss this." He nodded toward Holly, and normally she would wholeheartedly agree, but the circumstances today were anything but ordinary.

"It's the secret. Somehow Lillie found out that I want to wait, and she told Holly."

"Told *Holly*? This is crazy, sheer lunacy." His voice rose in agitation.

"I–I know, but it's true."

"Holly, please go upstairs and get started on your homework. I need to speak with Naomi."

"That's what I'm talking about. It's her, always her." Holly stomped her feet, fists curled at her side.

"Please, just give me a minute and then I'll check up on you, okay?" He leaned down and reached for her, but Holly slipped past him and headed for the stairs. She stopped short and shot Naomi a filthy look but then marched up the stairs, following Bryce's directions.

"Is it true? Is it true that you don't want to have our baby?"

"Of course it's not true. I want that more than anything but just not now. I mean, do you seriously think it's a good idea with that psychopath lingering around?" She pointed her finger toward the window where Lillie sat on the driveway, cuddling with Zelda.

He cast his head down and took a long moment before he lifted his gaze. "But what if this never ends? What then? Excuse me for saying this, but we just can't seem to catch a break."

"I—what do you want me to do? How do you think I feel, knowing this is all my fault? That if I didn't attract ghosts like white on rice our lives would be safe, normal?" Naomi paused, catching her breath, but with that she broke into tears. "I'm trying my best to talk to that little monster, but she's impossible, Bryce. She is an impossible brat!"

"Stop it. She's a kid, Naomi, a kid. You need to keep that in mind." But he softened a bit at the sight of her tears. "Shh, come here." He pulled her into his chest and rubbed her back. "Listen, maybe you've been too harsh on her, maybe that's why she hates you so much. You probably remind her of someone who treated her poorly, someone who she couldn't trust."

She considered his words and didn't entirely dismiss them. "You're right about that. It's her mother and father she despises, and I'm pretty sure she lumps me in with them just because I'm Holly's mother figure."

His fingers froze on her back and then he distanced himself from her. "Mother *figure*? *Figure*?"

She knew how the words must sound, but she swore she hadn't meant it. Not the way it came out. "I *am* her mother, Bryce, you know I am. Don't choose a time like this to mince my words. We're all under a lot of stress." Things seemed to be falling apart faster than she could do damage control.

Her hands shook as she tried to make him understand. "Bryce, please." It was all she could muster.

"I want to have another child, Naomi. I want your baby, *our* baby. This is among the most important wishes in my life."

"And don't you think I want the same? Give me time. That's all I need. I'm worried that she might harm our baby if I were to get pregnant now. She's capable of anything."

"I get it, but again, this may never end. And if it does finally end? Then who will be the next soul knocking on our door? Who will it be next time, Naomi? Who, Jack the Ripper?"

"That's not fair! Don't do this. Please don't do this to us." Her heart ached for her marriage, her family, her sanity.

"Well, we can't ignore the possibility, and what then?"

"I don't know." A rising sadness spread through her, bringing her down, crushing her dreams of the perfect little family. What did perfect family mean anyway? Hell, there was no perfect with Lillie here. They were a quirky little family even without the lurking ghosts and she didn't care. What she did care about was Bryce and Holly, and she was determined to prove it.

"I'll put a stop to her, mark my words." She turned and headed for the kitchen, determined to meet up with Lillie alone in the place where she had first found her.

Bryce called to her as she quickened her pace. "You're angry right now, this isn't a good idea. She's a child, Naomi, a child."

Really? His words didn't fall on deaf ears, but Lillie had a hell of a lot more experience manipulating people than all of the adults Naomi knew tied together.

"Where are you? Show yourself." She pulled the stove out from against the wall with minimal effort and crawled through the dark space, coughing at the rising dust.

*Are the two of you going to send me away?*

The haunting words echoed and bounced around Naomi's

head as she called out for Lillie. What did that mean?

"Lillie. Did they send you away somewhere? Did they send you to a relative's house? A boarding school?"

Quiet. So very quiet. Where was Lillie?

"There you are." Naomi edged upward as she heard a child's laughter. But then she stopped cold at the sound of something else.

Something different. A southern accent?

More than one voice.

Several.

"Who's there? Who is that?"

She heard snippets of a conversation, and then a child's voice, but distinctly male.

"*I'm hungry, Papa.*"

Sobs.

"*Shh, it won't be long now. They're only waiting it out.*"

"*But my belly hurts so much.*" More sobs.

What she witnessed next stole her breath away. Lillie knelt before a family and reached her hand out to touch the distended belly of a young boy, no more than six or seven years old. His mother, she presumed, dressed in a stained white smock of a dress and a head wrap, held the tiny boy in her arms, pressing sweet kisses over his dark skin as the father stood, pacing the dark passageway.

*What's this?* Naomi darted her eyes from one member of the family to the next. They all donned the tattered white, filthy clothes from years gone by.

"Hello?" Naomi called out, attempting to gain their attention, all the while knowing these individuals had long passed. Her fears were confirmed as she ran a hand over the woman's arm as her own seemed to slice right through it, an apparition of sorts.

Ghosts.

Slaves?

Ghosts of passengers from the Underground Railroad?

Spirits. More spirits, crossing her path. For what reason, she didn't know, but she strongly suspected they were tied into the importance of Lillie and her journey to despair.

"*Something's wrong, Maribel. I feel it.*" The words mere whispers to save the worry of the boy, she was sure, but as if in dream state, Naomi heard each word clearly.

"*They'll let us know when it's safe, they will. They're good people.*"

"*We're not going to get out of here alive. I love you. Remember that, my beautiful wife.*" Another whisper.

"*What is the matter with you? Now stop that nonsense. You're scaring the heck out of yourself and me. Now drink that water over here and hush.*" She handed her husband a dirt-stained cup.

"*Mama?*" The boy turned his tear-stained face toward his mother. "*Do you see her?*" The woman passed the water to her son.

"*See who?*"

"*Her. It's Lillie again.*"

"*You must be delirious, talking about that girl again. Now drink that water.*"

"*She makes me feel better, helps the pain go away,*" the boy said, holding out his hand for Lillie to grasp.

Naomi didn't move, wouldn't chance breaking the spell. She couldn't believe what played out before her and the selflessness displayed by Lillie. She cared deeply for this boy and his family.

"*Joshua,*" Lillie stated with a firm conviction. "*I'm here, and I'm not going anywhere. I have you, you hear? Now hold on tight."*

She could hear the panic cleverly contained in Lillie's tone. The air grew frigid as Naomi steeled herself for what would come next. She knew. Lillie *knew* the boy and family were in grave danger. Now, she distracted the boy and his weeping parents with a lullaby, Lillie's own sorrow barely contained as a tear spilled out and traveled down her cheek.

No, maybe everything would be okay. But Naomi heard the shout of men's voices and the screaming from a woman and man below, right in the kitchen.

*"Run! Run!" But she knew the family's fate had already been sealed, so very long ago.*

Why weren't they moving? Couldn't they at least try to get out from upstairs? It had to be worth a shot. Hell, if they didn't move, she would. Naomi stumbled to her feet, reaching out for Lillie, but the girl scarcely noticed her.

"Come on, follow me." As ridiculous as it seemed, she couldn't sit back and watch this scene play out before her without taking action. Who knows; maybe in this strange alternate plane, she could make a difference. She had to try.

Shots rang out from below as a woman's shrill scream cried out for what must be her husband. The only sound that followed was that of two men and their harrowing footsteps.

Naomi sprinted from step to step, not caring if she fell, right toward the wall upstairs, which provided the way out. She shoved her body, again, and again. It was of no use, almost as if it were sealed. They were trapped. She was trapped right along with them.

Back down the stairs she traveled, this time, knowing there could be no possible outcome other than the worst.

Lillie held the wailing boy's hands and then pulled him impossibly close as the men lifted their rifles and aimed.

Lillie then turned, locking her hopeless eyes with Naomi. *"It always goes like this."* Lillie's body then slumped forward with the weight of the family, like dominoes, falling against her, never breaking contact with the dying boy.

Naomi screamed out, knowing the chances the men could see her standing there were slim, but up went her hands, shielding her face as she prepared to take the brunt of the next shot from the men's dirt-stained rifles.

*"They're gone. Gone. They're all gone,"* Lillie *wailed uncontrollably as she rocked the boy back and forth, his eyes forever frozen in fear.*

"Lillie!" She reached for the girl, this time not caring about the consequences, but Lillie turned away and dropped her head atop the boy's lifeless form, shrugging Naomi's hand off her.

*"It always ends this way."* A river of tears slid down Lillie's face as her eyes pleaded for Naomi, as if asking her to go back and somehow change the outcome of events. It was then that finally, Naomi saw the innocent child that she was.

# CHAPTER NINE

Rᴇsᴇᴀʀᴄʜ. Sʜᴇ ᴄᴏɴᴅᴜᴄᴛᴇᴅ a grueling eight plus hour investigation at the library and clerk's office on the history of this town, and more specifically, the role this house and its former occupants played. She discovered that a husband, wife, and a family of runaway slaves had been murdered at her home in the mid-1800's. The facts didn't surprise her, given the age of the house, but what she needed to know was why the souls still lingered and what she could do to help them, as well as Lillie, find closure.

Bryce hadn't been thrilled when she shared her latest escapade with him in the passageway, but she had witnessed the mix of emotion as it played out across his face: anger, fear, concern, sorrow, and yes, eventually understanding.

After everything she had seen, Naomi had wrongly assumed that she could make some headway with Lillie. She couldn't have been more wrong, for each time Naomi had sought Lillie out, she was met with silence. Worse than that, the chandelier in the dining room had come inches away from landing on her head just yesterday. One thing became clear; Lillie's behavior wasn't going to change.

After she had spent hours at the library, Bryce had called her and asked if she would come home.

When she walked in the house and was in his arms, he rubbed her neck. "You need to rest. You've been at this for hours."

"You couldn't imagine the heartache that took place here, Bryce. *Here,* in this very house."

He released her and walked into the kitchen. Moments later, he returned with a grim look on his face and two glasses of wine in hand. "You can't keep rehashing this, it's not healthy. Here, have a glass of wine and sit." Bryce handed her a glass of her favorite Pinot Noir, she took a gulp, and then sat down as Bryce joined her.

"Where's Holly?"

"She's in bed for the night."

She realized she had stayed at the library until closing time. It was now after nine o'clock, far later than she realized.

A moment of uncomfortable silence filled the air. She didn't know what to say. If she went into detail about her findings, he would get annoyed. If she didn't, he would still be aggravated. Lately it seemed she couldn't win when it came to her ability to communicate effectively with Bryce.

"So?" Are you going to tell me what you found out?"

She exhaled and gripped her fingers around the stem of her wineglass. "Sure." She told him everything she had learned and then settled back to see how he would process the information.

"So that's it for now."

"I'm not surprised there's so much history here, and I'm sorry you had to go through that. It must have been difficult to witness." He steered the conversation back to what she told him about the passageway.

"Well, as awful as it was to watch it firsthand, I can only imagine how horrific it must be for Lillie to have had to witness it God only knows how many times. And she still goes back."

He squeezed her hand as a smile brightened his face. "Is that empathy I'm hearing for Lillie?"

"You know how I am with empathy. If anything is the problem, it's that I feel too much."

"Yes and no."

"What the hell is that supposed to mean?"

"It means that for some reason, this girl has gotten under your skin, like even Nick hadn't been able to."

She couldn't argue with that. "She's uncontrollable and is threatening my family. She's messing with Holly, for God's sake."

"I know but this softening toward her might be just what works when it comes to communicating with her."

He had a point. She had known plenty of children, her childhood self included, who didn't respond well to the tough love approach. She supposed what made it challenging on her part was the knowledge that although Lillie was a child to the naked eye, her years of existence as a spirit had hardened her so that it was difficult for her to see the little girl hiding inside.

"Okay, okay. I'll play along with that line of thinking for now."

"Just don't lose sight of the big picture here."

"Being?"

"Being that this is a child in distress looking for a way to right the wrongs that have been done to her, even if it means taking it out on total strangers who just happen to be inhabiting her home."

"I'm not a stranger. She sought me out as a child, don't forget that."

"I hear you, but try to relax a bit with her, at least for tonight?"

"Okay, but she's got anger issues. She's got the impulsivity of a child."

"She *is* a child."

"I know, I know. I mean, how are you remaining so calm, Bryce? She's using Holly!"

"You don't think I realize that? Don't you see the more you piss her off, talk bad about her, the worse she retaliates?"

"I guess, but it's like I'm stuck. I need to see this whole problem from a different perspective."

"*I'm* your different perspective."

"Yes, you are, but I need more. I need Lillie to calm down, to take a step back and think first without acting."

"Good luck with that."

"Then you know what?" She racked her brain, what could she do? Something had to give. "I need a break. If she won't do it, then I'll do it for the both of us."

"I'm not following."

"So remember when we went to Cape Florence?" The trip had given her a breather, even though the spirit world of Cape Florence was as active as a beehive.

"A vacation? You want to take a vacation? Now?"

"It couldn't hurt, and maybe Lillie needs to stew a bit and think about the consequences of her behavior."

"Like a time out?"

She chuckled at that. "Yes, I guess you could call it that." The more she thought this through, the better sense it made. If she, Bryce, and Holly weren't here in the house, she had no one left to play head games with and would have to sit and think, hopefully about the talk Naomi was about to have with her.

"But didn't you say she's followed you to the old mental facility? I mean what if she has the ability to transcend space? What if she comes with us?"

Why did Lillie show up both times she was helping Miriam? Lillie hadn't shown herself in any other distant location. There had to be a reason, and Naomi felt that reason on the tip of her tongue… close, but not close enough to grab.

"I don't think she will, but if she does, we deal with it. What do you say?" Her eyes pleaded with him as she did her best to convince him.

He didn't speak for a few moments, but she could tell her idea was growing on him. He grabbed hold of her and shook her arms. "Let's do it. Holly has been begging me to let her spend some time at my mom and dad's, and they've been doing the same. I didn't want to let her out of my sight with everything going on, but it could be the safest place for her right now, away from Lillie and–"

"Away from me." She finished his sentence but realized her feelings weren't hurt. He was right, this could be the best thing for all of them. A chance for Holly to escape this insanity, albeit temporarily, and an opportunity for Naomi and Bryce to work out the growing pains in their relationship.

"I didn't mean–"

"You did, but it's okay. You're right, Bryce."

"I am?"

"Yes. Let's do this." She grinned, taking hold of his arms. "Where to and when do we leave?"

"You're serious?"

"Absolutely. Give me some ideas."

"Well, as for when, Holly has a long weekend coming up, so would this coming weekend work? We could go for three or four nights?"

"Yes," she responded immediately, clasping her hands together. "Where?"

"Cape Florence?"

She figured it would be nice to see their friends Kristen and Jackson, who owned the bed and breakfast there, but then she thought of the appeal of going somewhere new. She made a face at his idea, turning her nose up. "As much as I love that place, we need someplace new, somewhere different."

"Okay, let's see." He went into his pacing mode and she took the time to think as well.

"I've got it!" She giggled with the exuberance of a child and ran to her office to grab a map of the United States she had curled away in her filing cabinet, the one she used to use for fleshing out a setting for her novels. When she first started writing, she would close her eyes, spin around, and place a push-pin into a random location–bam, the location of her next book. She hadn't used that strategy for developing her setting in years, but she remembered how much fun it was to grab hold of an unknown town, research it to death, and write away. If that was fun, she nearly jumped with excitement at how thrilling it would be to actually visit a random spot based purely on chance.

"What are you doing now?" Bryce groaned when he saw the map, but then a grin played on his face.

*Huh. He's enjoying this as much as I am,* Naomi mused. "Hold it out and I'll cover my eyes." She jumped in place, anxious to set the plan in motion.

"Whoa, hold on there. We only have a limited amount of time we can spend on our trip, so let's say we limit our search to the East Coast?"

"Party pooper." She expelled a breath, but the giggle returned. "Fine. Let's go. Hold out the map, and turn me around."

"I won't even ask where you got this idea from."

"Then zip it, and let's do this." She nearly squealed with excitement.

Feeling Bryce's hands spin her shoulders gently, she imagined where the southernmost section of the map would be. It would be nice to go somewhere warm, maybe the beach? Southern Florida? The Keys? She purposely drove her hands down as far as she could but was intercepted by Bryce, pushing the map upward.

"That's not fair, Bryce. Let me do this my way." She pointed her finger and felt the map rising a bit. "Bryce!" A giggle escaped as she pressed her pointer finger smack down on a spot and then opened her eyes.

"Florida." They both exclaimed simultaneously.

"Florida!" Naomi cried out as she jumped in place.

"Huh. Okay, so Florida it is."

Ends up it was northeast Florida to be exact. "Yes, we're off to a city called Augusta."

"Isn't that in Georgia?"

"Apparently there's an Augusta, Florida as well, and we're going." She flung her arms around his neck and kissed him.

"Are you sure we shouldn't research this a bit? Is it even near the beach?" He leaned his head toward the map, squinting his eyes.

"Right on the coastline, no worries."

"No worries."

The phrase *famous last words* came to mind, but she threw the negativity aside and concentrated on her next course of action. "I'll handle the hotel, you take care of the airline?"

"Sure. I should call my parents and make sure the dates work for them first, but yeah, I'm kind of looking forward to this."

"*Kind of?*" she teased right back.

She opened her mouth with another retort, but he silenced her with a kiss. Yeah, she really needed this trip.

# CHAPTER TEN

THERE WERE SOME last minute items to attend to, which included meeting up with Miriam and the victim's brother, Cole, at Miriam's house. They had just sat down to have coffee when there was a knock on the door. Miriam got up to answer the door and showed him into the kitchen.

Naomi had led Miriam on the scent of the ex-husband as the primary suspect in Sharon Wilde's murder, and she assumed they would try to see if she could give them any more information to support the theory.

"Hi Naomi. I'm Cole."

"Sorry to meet you under such circumstances. I'm sorry for your loss."

"Thank you, and thanks for your help with the case as well. Miriam speaks highly of you."

Naomi narrowed her eyes and thought she saw a slight pink color rise to Miriam's cheeks. "Hm–she does?"

"She does," Miriam responded as her color deepened a bit more.

"So what do you guys need from me?" Naomi was anxious to start packing and finalizing details for her upcoming trip.

"I heard your suspicions, and I feel strongly that you might be right. Sharon tried to hide the fact that Barry had a volatile temper, but we saw it. We all knew."

"How so?"

"Telltale signs of abuse, but that was only near the end. In the beginning, it was the look in her eye when he approached, like she worried that one of us might say something to piss him off. Later, she would make excuses not to show up at parties, you know how it is. Finally, she admitted the ass had been verbally abusing her, robbing her of her self-confidence."

"Did he ever hit her?" It was helpful to know these things, to put together the big picture.

"She denied it, but I wasn't convinced. A guy like that rarely knows where to draw the line."

Smart. Cole seemed solid and not bad on the eyes, either. She could have smacked herself as she remembered the reason why they were all standing here. His poor sister had been murdered, and here she was admiring the guy's handsome looks. Glancing at Miriam, she paused. It seemed her friend had noticed the shaggy dark blond hair and bronze eyes as well.

Damn, Miriam's cheeks burned more scarlet by the second. Naomi could hardly keep her jaw from hitting the floor.

Miriam snapped out of her daze and mumbled something Naomi didn't catch, at least, not while she was pondering over the look on Miriam's face.

"Naomi? Earth to Naomi?" Miriam's impatient tone warned Naomi to stop staring.

"Yes." She swallowed her grin.

"Can you pick up on anything else? Anything at all?"

She wished she could deliver better news to Cole, but then she had a thought. "Bring me to her house. Her happy place."

Some unsettled spirits gravitated toward the place of death, while others clung to the places that'd once given them peace and security.

"It's right down the street from here. You guys can come with me or follow me."

Miriam and Cole locked eyes, and Naomi suddenly felt as if she were the third wheel. "I have a lot to do. How about I follow you guys, and then I can take off when I'm done?"

"Okay, sounds fine to me. Let's go, Miriam."

Naomi gulped the last of her coffee, slammed the mug in the sink, and then trailed behind Miriam and Cole. Miriam turned around for a split second and offered up the most mischievous grin Naomi had ever seen from her friend. Something was brewing here. Miriam was behaving like a teenager, smack in the middle of a murder case.

The house was actually right down the street, less than five minutes away. The short ride gave Naomi time to unwind and clear her thoughts. It always helped when she wiped the clutter from her mind before trying to connect with the spirit world.

Upon arriving at Sharon's home, Naomi felt nothing strange or unusual. The walkway up to the front door was still tidy and neat, and the lawn had obviously been attended to recently. Cole studied her and proved again how sharp he was.

"Did you–"

"I've tried to keep up with basic things around here, mowing the lawn, grabbing her mail you know."

"Hey," Miriam interjected. "I'm the detective here, and we've already covered this." She threw her hands up wide, gesturing to their surroundings.

"Yeah, just trying to help."

"Right this way. Watch your step." Cole unlocked the door with his key and switched the hallway light on. Naomi glanced around the living room, taking in the blue sofa and coffee table. Save for one magazine, the table was clear of clutter. Same for the kitchen. Not one dish littered the sink, and a lemon fresh smell filled the air.

"Was she always this neat, or is this your touch in here as well?"

Miriam locked eyes with Cole. The two seemed to share some secret piece of information. "She used to be a downright slob, but it seems Barry changed that about her. Every time I came here, there wouldn't be anything out of place, not one dish in the sink."

If it were her, she would revert back to her messy ways once she left the ass, but everyone had their own way of dealing with their issues, she supposed. Next, Naomi asked to see any recent photographs. The one Miriam had shown her from the police station gave her a general idea of what Sharon Wilde looked like physically, but Naomi wished to see more of her personality, get a true feel for what Sharon had been like.

Miriam helped Cole scoop up some framed photos from around the room. Most of them showed an attractive woman with dirty blonde hair and brown eyes. She looked quite a bit like her brother.

"The dog. Where's the dog from this picture?" Sharon had her arms draped over a large German Shepard somewhere outdoors, perhaps a park.

"Sam? Oh, he's staying with me."

Her mind ticked away, delving into possibilities. "Sam, he must have been here, though, right? I mean, you know, the last time she left the house."

"Or was taken from the house, more like. It's doubtful that she would have willingly left with Barry at this point in their relationship."

True, he had a point. "Have you swept the area?"

A glaring Miriam barked her response, "Are you serious?"

"Yes, of course you would have." She should have known better than to try to ask Miriam if she had completed her job. She and her partner were on top of every minute detail when it came to crime scenes.

"And–nothing?"

"His fingerprints were all over the house, but I wouldn't expect anything else. He lived here not too long ago and had visited Sharon several times since they had separated."

"He was a persistent son of a bitch, that's for sure," Cole remarked, shaking his head as his eyes scanned the living room and kitchen beyond.

"Show me her bedroom."

"Right up here." Cole led the way down the hallway of the small ranch and into the master bedroom. A faint feeling of nausea rose within her, and she stepped back, leaning against the wall for support.

"You okay?" Miriam stepped toward her, reaching for Naomi's hand.

"I–" Naomi attempted to speak before she saw a vision spring before her. A vision of Sharon and a man that must be

Barry, sharing a bed. Better times, from what she could see but then another image of arguing, a hand placed up to her cheek as Sharon grabbed it. Barry twisted her wrist, chuckling as Sharon gasped, writhing in pain. Naomi clutched her own wrist, tears escaping as she cried out loud.

"Naomi!"

*Not now, Miriam, not now.* Another nightmare came to life, stealing her breath.

*"What are you doing here?! You can't be here—leave!"*

*"Not a chance." He glanced around, taking in the nightstand littered with make-up and a curling iron."*

*"I'm sorry. Am I interrupting something? Are you going on a date?"*

*"Leave. I want you to leave immediately."*

*"Is this a date? Are you freaking kidding me? Already? My side of the bed isn't even cold, and off you go looking to sleep around?"*

*"No, it's not that."*

*"Liar, liar, you women are such liars. Who is he? I'll kill him. I will. Tell me who he is."*

*"Barry, you need to stop." Sharon eyed the door to the bedroom as she edged her way toward it, but her ex was too quick.*

*"You're hurting me. Let go of me."*

*His hand shot out, grabbing a fistful of hair. Naomi wished she could turn away, but she had to see how this played out, no matter how hard it was, no matter what it took from her.*

*"You are not going on a date. You are not going to even have coffee with another man. I won't allow it."*

*Sharon howled in pain but managed to escape from Barry's grasp. "Sharon!" He sprinted after her, his gait longer than hers. She heard the thunderous sound of a freight train approaching* in the distant part of her consciousness, but she brushed the pesky detail aside.

He was on her heels, inching closer as she pulled the front door open, crying out for anyone to here. But then, why hadn't neighbors reported sounds of a struggle? Sharon's screams? The freight train's obnoxious, piercing horn sounded not once, not twice, but four times. Four whistles, each one sealing Sharon's fate.

A thought hit her as she, herself, searched frantically around the space of her vision. Where was the dog? Where was Sam? She should have heard barking at least.

"Sam? Sam?" It was if Naomi had read Sharon's mind, and unfortunately Naomi knew Sharon's mistake moments before she made it.

Naomi glanced across the yard at a dozing Sam with slivers of a bone by his side. Barry must have drugged the dog.

"Sam!" Sharon spun her head, taking in the sight of the dog, hesitating for just a moment, but it was long enough for Barry to take charge of the situation. He tackled her, slamming the full weight of his body on top of her slender frame. His arms moved quick, pinning her down with one hand and silencing her cries with his other.

"He'll be fine, but I'm not sure I can say the same for you." He kept his hands firmly on her mouth, and Naomi winced as she took in Sharon's wide, bulging eyes. He dragged her flailing body to his car, opened the passenger side door, hesitated, and then hit her squarely across the jaw. Naomi howled, feeling fear, pain, and an aching throb of hopelessness.

"He brought her to the abandoned hospital. He was here. He took her from her own home."

"Here?" Cole's hands went to Naomi, steadying her shaking body.

"Nobody saw her. It was dark, she was getting ready to go out on a date. Nobody heard her—the train came at precisely the moment he dragged her kicking and screaming out of the house."

With that, Naomi fell to her knees, clutching her pounding head. Her empathetic abilities took more of a toll on her lately, each time she tapped into another's emotions. Her head—it throbbed, and her heart—ached.

# CHAPTER ELEVEN

Everything appeared to be in order. Each bag she needed was packed and waiting by the stairs. The only thing bothering her was Zelda. Since the cat had recently taken to bonding with Lillie, she and Zelda had become more distant, and it bothered the hell out of her. It wasn't as if Zelda ignored her completely, but when she had the choice to be with either her or Lillie, the little ghost always won Zelda's affections. She had left enough food and refilled Zelda's bowl with fresh water. When Bryce's parents had stopped over to pick up Holly, they had assured Naomi they would drop by each day to feed Zelda and give her fresh water.

"She'll be fine." Bryce read her mind and placed a gentle hand on her shoulder.

"I suppose." It wasn't food or water she worried about, rather it was leaving Zelda in the hands of that little terror. But, Naomi had to admit that Lillie appeared just as fond of the cat as it was of her.

"Ready?" Bryce grabbed her waist and spun her around to face him. "We have a flight to catch. Are you coming or not?"

She kissed him quickly on the lips and glanced around the room. All was in order. Even Lillie remained silently cooperative. "Take good care of Zelda, you hear me, Lillie?"

She hadn't expected a response, and she didn't receive one. Figures, she would remain elusive when Naomi needed something from her.

"Let's go, Naomi." Bryce nudged her toward the door, and Naomi set her mind on one thing only, having a relaxing long weekend.

AFTER AN UNEVENTFUL flight and cab ride from the airport to their hotel, Naomi gazed around the lobby of the hotel in appreciation. The high, decorative ceilings and paintings that adorned nearly every square inch of the walls gave the feeling that one was in a museum rather than a hotel. The Spanish Colonial architecture of this building, and a host of others in the small city, cried out for visitors to wander every inch of the town. Upon arriving, Naomi had tugged Bryce, exclaiming over the beauty of the city, making mental notes of the places she wished to visit once they unpacked and settled into their room.

"Here's a complimentary voucher for a glass of sangria." Nothing sounded better at that moment. Florida, Bryce, and a glass of sangria, what else could she ask for?

"Is there someone who can tell us which sites are the best

to visit? We're only here for a few nights." Naomi's mind was already out on the streets beyond, wanting to fill their mini-vacation with the distractions she so desperately needed.

"Naomi, how about we settle in for a bit? Then we'll come down and make a plan?"

"How many nights are you here for?" The receptionist behind the desk busied herself reaching for some papers.

"Three," Naomi replied.

"Here, you must do one of our ghost tours. There's a zillion companies and tours, but in my opinion, this one is the best."

"Ghost tours?" Naomi and Bryce spoke at once, their eyes wide.

"Haven't you heard? Augusta is one of the oldest cities in the country and also one of the most haunted."

A small grin crept across Naomi's face as Bryce gazed down at the floor and cursed.

"WHAT ARE THE chances, Naomi? I mean really."

The sun had gone down after an afternoon spent exploring their hotel, the attached art gallery, and the grounds, which included a dramatic pool area, complete with outdoor couches, beds, and a smattering of bright white romantic lights around the perimeter of the space.

"Look over there," Naomi said, spying yet another architectural dream. The entire city of Augusta sparkled, lit up for what the hotel clerk said was their beloved annual event. She had seriously never seen a place that even came close to rivaling this in her life. The attention to detail in this city was impeccable, not only was every building alight, but strings of light popped out everywhere the eye could see.

"I feel like we're in some kind of fairy tale, like a wonderland." She spun her head around, trying to take it all in. "This has to be one of the most romantic spots in the country."

The lights from the city sparkled in Bryce's eyes. "When you're here, it is."

"Aw." She squeezed his hand and kissed him on the mouth but then became distracted by her surroundings.

"Look—the woman at the front desk said these two buildings had once been majestic hotels where the rich and famous used to play."

"Wow, I have to admit this place is amazing." Bryce whistled under his breath, taking in the view.

"Right? I mean can you believe we lucked out like this? From me just randomly picking this place on the map?"

"Naomi, nothing with you is random. What are the chances we're in one of the most haunted spots in the U.S.?"

True. It was true.

"Should we do it tonight?" She nearly squealed aloud. He raised his brows in question. "The tour, Bryce, the ghost tour."

"Really? Do you even need to book a tour? Ghosts all flock to you anyway. Hell, you should be the tour. We could charge people to follow you around. They'd get a show for sure, one they wouldn't soon forget."

"Come on, that's not funny."

"Not funny… but true."

"Fine, let's do it, though. I feel like a sponge here in this city. I just want to soak up the history of everything around me. I want to hear all the old stories this city has to tell."

"Need I remind you that we came here for a break from all this ghost business?"

She recalled their past getaway to Cape Florence and her encounter with the spirit that resided in their inn. She hadn't gotten much of a break there either, but she had received some insight into the workings of another haunted soul, which had ultimately opened her mind more to her problems at hand.

She pulled him toward the information booth nestled to the side of the cobblestoned pedestrian mall. Bryce sighed, and although she did have to drag him into the tiny building, in the end, he went along with her, and they found themselves visiting the proclaimed haunted sites, such as the small graveyard where soldiers were said to be buried several bodies deep to each grave, the old jail, and more. In each location, Naomi felt a prickle of energy, but it was difficult to open her mind to the environment with so many other tourists walking beside her.

"Well?" Bryce pulled her in close and kissed her cheek when they found themselves outside after the tour ended. "Have you had enough?"

"I guess, but I couldn't connect to much because of the interference of so many people."

"You sound disappointed."

"A little," she admitted. "Listen, you remember Millie, from Cape Florence?"

"Of course." The spirit had connected with Bryce, asking in her own mystical way for him to protect Naomi.

"Didn't you feel she supported us?"

"Is that what you're looking for? Support? *I'm* your support. I got you, Naomi."

"I know you do, but—oh, just forget it." She couldn't

make him understand what didn't come naturally for him.

"Hungry?"

Although it was late, they hadn't had a chance to grab more than a slice of pizza all day; a slice of the most delicious pizza she had ever tasted she noted. "I'm famished. Too bad that pizza place is across town."

Most of the city's attractions were within walking distance to each other, but the tour had dropped them off on the outskirts of town, and the taxis were booked up to an hour.

"Pizza? Come on, we can do better than pizza."

"Yes, but you have to admit that pizza was pretty amazing."

"It was, but look, I heard this place is one of the best restaurants in town."

She gazed up at an old Victorian style building and nodded her head in agreement. "Henry's it is."

Turned out Henry's was delicious, and the setting couldn't have been more perfect. They ate outside on the second floor balcony, overlooking the bay. Staring out at the bridge dotted with the lights of traffic, Naomi realized she hadn't felt so relaxed in weeks. Her mind had finally been forced to let go of thoughts of ghosts, hauntings, and all of her recent stress. Instead, she basked in the tropical feel of the city and her husband beside her.

"Do you want another glass of wine, or should we head back to the hotel?"

"As tempting as another glass of wine sounds right now, I think we should check on that taxi and head back. The pool stays open for a while longer. What do you say we use our free sangria vouchers and hang by the pool before heading in for the night?"

"Sounds like a plan."

Smiling widely, she leaned over and kissed Bryce. "Just give me a minute? I have to run to the ladies room."

"Hurry back."

Naomi made her way back inside the second floor dining area and found her way to the bathroom. She checked her appearance in the antique mirror and then stopped to admire the décor of the room. From the old restored furniture to the lace doilies and intricate curtains, she felt as if she were thrown back to another era. She wiped the sheen of sweat from her forehead and headed into one of the stalls.

At first, she barely heard the chatter from outside her stall, but then a woman's voice grew louder, more insistent. Strange thing was Naomi only heard the one voice. She must be on her cell phone, Naomi thought. It wasn't until Naomi exited the stall that she saw the lady who stood speaking.

The woman, clad in a cotton dress and wide bonnet, wasn't on her phone at all, she was talking directly to Naomi. Prickles traveled across Naomi's skin, warning her that this wasn't someone dressed up for a museum tour or costume party. The spirit's features dropped, her eyes wide and accusing.

Rooted to the spot where she stood, Naomi opened her mouth to speak, but no words came.

"Beware the ancient souls." Her hands shook fiercely.

"Beware the innocent, for her power is too much, so strong." The voice boomed louder.

"I—" Naomi attempted before she was silenced with a shaking, wrinkled finger. Frigid fingertips traced her lips, preventing her from speaking, asking any questions.

"Beware." The ghost opened her mouth to bellow a silent scream, heard not by the human ear but surely by those in the spirit world, as windows flew open and curtains billowed, dancing with the haunting silence. Naomi spun around, glancing at the door, looking for her way out.

As if she had dreamed the apparition, the ghostly form instantly vanished, leaving just the breeze from the open windows and an unnatural chill in its wake. She stood, her mind whirring with question after question. Beware of what? Who? The innocent? Had this spirit been speaking of Lillie? Because Naomi needed answers, she waited it out, using her mind to try to summon the woman back here.

"Naomi?" Her focus broke as she heard Bryce knocking upon the door. Damn. Bryce peeked through the door and then opened it wider, slipping in. "Are you okay?"

"I–um." Before she had a chance to respond, the door opened again.

"Excuse me." The hostess she recognized from the upstairs dining room brushed past Bryce then stopped short at the sight of Naomi. "What's the matter, miss?"

She must have looked quite the sight, standing there, speechless. A look of understanding swept over the hostess's face. "Ah, did you have the pleasure of meeting Eloise?"

"Who?" Naomi nearly choked on the word.

"Eloise. Our resident spirit. She spends most of her time in this bathroom here."

Naomi locked eyes with Bryce as he yet again cursed openly.

"You've seen her?"

"Seen her? Heck, one of the local ghost tours actually comes right into this room as part of the tour. It's more like who hasn't seen her."

"Does she speak? Have you ever heard her speak?" She had to know if the phrases the ghost spat out held meaning or if they were just gibberish.

"Speak? No, Eloise has never spoken in all the years she's haunted this building. She stands silently, eloquently, in her fancy dress and bonnet, always the lady."

"Are you okay? Did she speak to you?"

"No," she dismissed the hostess, not wanting to cause alarm. In her mind, though, alarm bells went off at full speed. *Beware of the ancient. Beware of the innocent.*

"Let's get out of here." Bryce took her by the arm, guiding her out the door and down the stairs to the exit where the cabdriver sat waiting for them.

Naomi didn't speak a word until they got out of the cab and made their way into their hotel. "What a day, huh?"

"Maybe we should just call it a night," Bryce said, his eyes filled with concern.

"No, we'll have our sangrias by the pool but no more ghost talk tonight, okay?" Something about the words the ghost had spoken disturbed Naomi; the simple message to beware of what must be Lillie weighed heavily on Naomi. Had Lillie been there in the bathroom with them? Or was her spirit strong enough to transcend through to Eloise? Either possibility frightened the hell out of Naomi.

"You don't have to ask *me* twice." Bryce exhaled and headed to the bar to order their drinks.

# CHAPTER TWELVE

THE NEXT DAY started out well enough, as Naomi and Bryce enjoyed a quick breakfast and then went back to the room to put on their sunscreen before heading out into the heat of the day. Bryce stood, pressing the elevator button in the lobby for the third time.

"What's up with this elevator?" They had been standing there for a few minutes, and with everything that had been on her mind, Naomi barely noticed the wait.

"There," Naomi said, pointing to the doorway across the hall. "Let's just take the stairs."

She led the way into the stairwell, taking notice of the spiral stairs and colorful artwork that covered the walls. "Even the staircase is stunning in this place."

Bryce nodded his head in agreement and followed one step behind her. As they climbed the stairway, Naomi's mind went to the hidden stairwell back at their house. Her mind instantly filled with images of the runaway slaves, Lillie, and all their pain. She nearly tripped over a young woman who sat on one of the steps that wound up to their floor.

"Oh, excuse me."

"Who are you talking to?" Bryce chuckled from behind her and she stopped in her tracks.

From behind she saw that the woman sitting on the steps had short, jet-black hair, but she hadn't turned her head to face Naomi. Bryce went to move around Naomi, heading straight for the woman.

"Be careful!" But she watched as he walked right through the young woman. Not again. Naomi's pulse picked up as she stood, unable to move.

At last, the woman turned to face her, her heavily made up eyes rimmed with tears. "Save her, save her. It's too much. Save her, or get out. Go back home, go back home!"

Naomi swallowed. "Who? Save who?" She had to find out more. She couldn't turn from this spirit whom Bryce hadn't had the pleasure of seeing.

"Her. Save her, or get out!" she repeated, her voice echoing and booming from the walls.

Bryce grabbed for Naomi, but she hastily brushed him off. She needed to deal with this and get some answers. "Bryce—go, go back to the room, now."

"Hell no. I'm not going anywhere."

Dammit. She tuned him out. "Who? Are you talking about Lillie? Is that who you're talking about?"

"You don't know? How could you not know?"

"I do. It's Lillie, right?"

"My God—look, *look in the mirror*."

Searching the stairway for a mirror, she was stumped. "There's no mirror, what mirror?" Was Lillie there? Standing behind her? Out of Naomi's view, playing games?

"Wake up, and help her. It's you, she needs you."

With that last statement, she vanished. Just like Eloise. What was up with these ghosts? Why couldn't they simply tell her what was on their minds?

She turned to face Bryce. "Did you hear her? Did you hear what she said?"

"God help us both, Naomi." Bryce sighed heavily. "No, I did not hear her, nor did I see her, but I can tell you I think this may not have been the best place for us to come. They're freaking all over the place." He ran a hand through his hair, his face twisted with emotion.

"Exactly. Like you said before, nothing is random with me. We're here for a reason. They're helping me, helping us. It's like they're feeding me clues, and the sooner I solve this mystery, the sooner we can get back to our lives, back to normal."

"Normal? Normal, you say?" He offered up a skeptical nod of his head and led the way down the stairs to the lobby.

So IT WASN'T exactly a relaxing trip, but it was turning out to be an eventful one for sure. Last night, she had dreamed of the abandoned mental facility, but instead of seeing Sharon Wilde's face there, it was the face of Lillie. Lillie, who had sat on the floor of what appeared to be a hospital, doll in hand, wailing for her mother, over and over, until Naomi woke, covered in sweat. Bryce had slept through her tossing and turning, and each time she tried to go back to sleep, another dream blasted her with random events, clues, or both, she couldn't decipher, couldn't make sense out of any of it. Sharon Wilde eventually made her own appearance, begging her to take notice of the little things.

Taking notice of the little things had been advice she'd adhered to before, when working on Maggie, Ryan, and Nick's cases. Was it just the old, wise words streaming through her subconscious, or had she and Miriam missed something?

With last night now behind her, she and Bryce stood at the bottom floor of the Augusta Lighthouse, waiting for their nighttime ghost tour to begin.

"You are a glutton for punishment."

Ha. "So what if I am." She reached for his hand and squeezed it tightly while listening to the tour guide speak of the history of the lighthouse, as he took them through the living quarters of the old building, complete with the tales of various ghosts that had reportedly been seen and heard on the grounds throughout the years. The one that captured her attention the most involved a tale of a young girl sitting atop the lighthouse alone, in a long, flowing dress.

"Watch your step," the tour guide instructed. "The lighting is dim." The rest of the tour group gasped and giggled as they watched one in a group of three girls joke around with her friends. Naomi couldn't shake the story of the young girl at the top of the lighthouse, perhaps because Lillie, too, had been so young.

"You doing okay?" Bryce steadied her with his hand, using the other to shine his flashlight app as they ascended the steep stairs.

What he really wanted to know was if she had seen or felt anything unusual, and so far she wasn't picking up on any spirits. She felt herself begin to get winded as they got ready to climb the next set of stairs. "Hold up, I need to sit for a minute." She found a spot to sit near a single window, which overlooked the now dark grounds outside. She took a minute to catch her breath as Bryce chuckled.

"Out of shape?"

"Shut up. You work outdoors for a living. How many steps did the tour guide say in all?" She sighed, glancing upward.

"Only 219." He laughed openly.

"Only 219," she repeated. "Just wonderful."

Bryce reached his hand out for her to take and helped her up. "Come on, we need to catch up with the group."

"Fine, fine," Naomi grumbled, but she had to admit this was the kind of stuff she thrived on, being in a dark, haunted lighthouse with the man she loved.

Up, up, up, they went, and gradually Naomi started picking up stamina. Maybe it was the desire to catch up to the tour guide so that she could hear the spooky tales he spun about the previous owners, workers, and their families. The guide had the rest of the group outside on the top of the lighthouse when they finally caught up. Again, he spoke of the many stories, the footsteps neighbors heard, the haunted cemetery beyond the grounds, but when he zeroed back to the tale of the young girl who was seen sitting on the top of the lighthouse, she focused on hearing every word he spoke.

"Nobody knows much about that one, other than what they've seen. Based on the information from the sightings, she appears to be young, with a billowing white dress. She never turns around, so no one has actually seen her face."

"Has she ever spoken?" Naomi interjected.

"Spoken?"

"Yes, has she?"

"I don't recall hearing much about any of the spirits actually speaking, no. Some have reported footsteps being heard, some laughter, maybe something about singing, but no, no one has had an actual conversation with the ghosts." The comment earned a chuckle of laughter from the group.

Naomi felt the support of Bryce's hand on her arm as the group headed back inside the lighthouse. She hesitated as Bryce stood in the doorway, ready to head back down. "Give me a minute?"

Bryce nodded, remaining where he stood. "Sure."

"Alone?" She felt something shift in the air, the temperature, the energy? She couldn't be sure, but she wanted time alone out here to see if anything came to her.

"You sure?"

"Yes, I'll be right there. Promise."

For a moment she stood in the light of the moon, just stood, admiring the view of the moonlit beach beyond, enjoying the feel of the breeze running through her hair. She walked around the edge of the tower, and at first sight, it appeared another person from the tour had been left behind, but then she looked closer and noted the way this person sat near the railing, legs dangling precariously over the edge. "Be careful," Naomi called out, making her way closer.

But the girl didn't respond to her, nor did she turn to see where the voice had come from. "What—" Naomi bit back her words and remained still, for she knew from experience that the spirits could vanish in an instant when they wished to.

She didn't know if she should speak or not, so she did the latter, and instead, took in the image of precisely what the tour guide had spoken of moments earlier. Whomever had relayed their accounts of this vision had been spot on, for the young girl just sat, back turned, hair blowing in the wind as her feet dangled over the edge of the lighthouse.

Closer and closer, Naomi made her way toward the girl until she stood nearly a foot behind her, close enough to touch her if she wished, but she didn't dare. Although this girl was indeed a spirit, she didn't want to spook her, couldn't bear to see her fall off the edge. What else had the tour guide spoken of downstairs before they made their way up the steep, winding, cold steps? Yes, he had stated that the girl had been the daughter of one of the workers from the late 1800's, and that she had disobeyed her parents and climbed up to the top of the lighthouse, over the railing, peered over the edge and then scooted further still until she was seconds away from falling. Naomi clutched her throat as she realized that she hadn't known any of the specifics until that exact moment, somehow she knew the details and was now seeing it play out before her very eyes.

"No, don't–don't do that." Should she try to grab her or would that make it worse?

Time robbed her of a response as the girl ever so slowly turned her head so that Naomi could see the green in her young eyes, her upturned mouth, the white of her teeth. Her eyes, although young, had seen far too much pain, pain that Naomi now swallowed up as her own.

"You're too close to see, but open your eyes," the spirit whispered.

"Stop. Don't go any closer." She held her hand out, not caring what clues this girl had decided to share about Lillie but rather wanting to somehow stop the horrific course of events she knew she was powerless to control.

"It's beautiful out there, isn't it?" The girl's smile made Naomi cringe as she threw her tiny arms wide, gesturing toward the view beyond.

Naomi clutched her stomach, tamping down the rising bile. "No, don't go any further, please," she begged.

"She's in danger."

"Who? Lillie?"

A cryptic laugh followed, one that sunk its way to her core. "Who? Who?" Dread seeped through her limbs, cementing her to the spot where she stood, for she knew the answer already.

"Look closer. Look in your heart." She smiled openly, and Naomi saw the scared little girl flash before her but only for an instant.

"Who's in danger? Tell me!" Now Naomi didn't fight the rumbling in her belly or the tears that sprang to life.

"Why Holly, of course." The girl maintained eye contact, her gaze serious, as Naomi sank to the floor, helpless to change the action she knew this girl would take next, helpless to save Holly from the clutches of Lillie.

"It's beautiful out there, isn't it?" she repeated as she switched gears and edged her bottom impossibly over the railing.

"No!"

But before Naomi could even attempt to stand, the girl disappeared from sight as Naomi screamed for her, and for Holly. She was too late to help this poor girl, but as she heard the echoes of the girl's scream grow fainter, she stood with the strength she had inwardly conjured, feeling a renewed purpose.

She was too late to help this girl, and she might be too late to save Lillie's soul, but she wasn't too late to save Holly.

"Naomi, what is it?" At the sound of her screaming Holly's name, Bryce had come running. "What about

Holly? Is she okay?" He ran toward her, grabbing her arms, squeezing them tight, too tight.

"I think she's fine, but call your parents right now, and tell them that whatever they do, don't take Holly to our house." A stupefied Bryce stared, his mouth opened to speak.

"Do it! Do it now!"

His shaking hands scrambled for his cell phone, and she watched in fear as the call went to voicemail. What time was it? It was after dark, so maybe Holly was settled in bed, safe and sound at her grandparents' house.

"Come on, come on!" Bryce's voice rose to hysteria. As his fingers bore down on his phone in a vain attempt to reach his parents, he finally sank to the floor and cried out. "What's happening, Naomi? What's happening to Holly?"

"Get up, Bryce. This is no time to give up. Get off your butt, and let's go." She pulled him by the hand and led him down the stairs, not caring about the glances they earned or the shouts from the tour guide to be careful. With one hand on the railing and one hand on her cell phone, Naomi dialed the number of the taxi service, wishing they had rented a car instead.

"Ten minutes, the car will be here in ten minutes." Bryce didn't respond but kept trying his parents. They had finally exited the lighthouse and had nothing to do but wait for their ride.

"Dammit, dammit!" Bryce threw his cell down on the grass. "What happened up there?" She bent down to pick up his cell and considered her next words.

"I–it's more of a feeling."

"Bullshit, Naomi. Tell me!"

As she recounted the details of her interaction with the girl who went over the edge of the lighthouse, she watched as Bryce's face transformed to pure terror. Reaching for his hand, she met his resistance and backed away.

This wasn't good. The ache in her gut told her it wasn't, and she wasn't one to ignore her gut. If something happened to Holly, Naomi couldn't imagine how she would ever deal with it, and thinking about how she felt only made her heart ache for Bryce that much more.

That girl knew something. How she knew was beyond Naomi, but she did know something, just like the others in this spirit-riddled city. She rubbed at her goosebumps as she glanced up at the lighthouse, already knowing what she would see. The girl was up there once more, perched on the edge of the lighthouse, inching closer to the edge, destined to relive the horror that ended her life again and again, not unlike the slaves in the passageway. She shuddered and turned away, refusing to watch this scene a second time.

Once back at the hotel, while Bryce continued to try his parents, Naomi arranged for a red-eye flight back to New York. He didn't speak more than a few necessary words to her until the flight touched down in New York, and she hadn't expected him to.

"Bryce–" she finally attempted. At that precise moment, Bryce's cell rang as her heart leaped with hope.

"What? What did you say? No! Where is she? Where is she? Oh my God, did you call the police?" His hands shook furiously as Naomi turned away. This was all her fault. *All her fault*, but blaming herself right now would only slow down what she needed to do, and that was act. Her mind was already on it, already formulating a plan because, for lack of other options, what else could she do?

# CHAPTER THIRTEEN

WHILE THE POLICE, including Miriam, scoured every square inch of first their house, and then the grandparents' house, she replayed the story Bryce's parents told of coming here after ice cream to feed Zelda and to grab one of Holly's stuffed animals. The grandparents swore Holly wasn't out of their sight for more than an instant, only when she had asked to go to the bathroom on the second floor. That was where she had disappeared. Holly's grandfather had been right in Holly's bedroom, and upon hearing the toilet flush, came out to wait for her to emerge from the bathroom. He claimed he heard two distinct children's voices, and she believed him.

Shadows etched under the eyes of Bryce and his parents, their faces too unbearable to look at. Worse than that was the distance Bryce put between them, and she knew if it were her, she'd do exactly the same. She did have to speak to him though.

"I'm going to go somewhere else tonight. I'll have my cell on me if you need me. I'm sorry, Bryce, and I'm here for you."

She couldn't be sure he even heard a word she'd muttered, but she gathered a pillow and blanket, along with her cell phone, and made her way to the hidden passageway. The cops had been in here as well but had found nothing. No surprise, Lillie was as elusive as they came. But where would she hide Holly and how?

Hour after hour, she sat in vigil as she waited Lillie out. No amount of calling, pleading, or begging had enticed Lillie to show her smug little face. Naomi had offered herself over in exchange for Holly, but she knew the little spirit wanted Holly because that was the most painful revenge she could execute.

Revenge for what, though? What was it that Lillie thought she had done to deserve this torture?

It must have been close to two in the morning when Bryce texted her.

*I need time to think. I need you to leave me alone for a while, please.*

Her heart sank and ached for his forgiveness, forgiveness she knew she wouldn't give herself.

*You got it, but know that I'm not giving up on Holly.*

Or you, she wanted to write, but she held back the comment. Now wasn't the time for that.

As she sat, fighting the sleep that would ultimately come, Naomi pictured Bryce, lying in bed, his heart breaking, piece by piece, and for each break she felt his suffering and her own, melded together in a knot too painful to untie. Her soul tethered to his and to Holly's, and would be forever, regardless of how this mess unfolded.

She strained her memory to recall the exact words all of the spirits of Augusta had muttered.

*Beware the ancient souls.*

*Beware the innocent, for her power is too much, so strong.*

*Look closer. Look in your heart.*

*You're too close to see, but open your eyes.*

*You don't know? How could you not know?*

*Save her, save her. It's too much. Save her, or get out. Go back home, go back home.*

*My God–look. Look in the mirror.*

*Wake up, and help her.*

*It's you. She needs you.*

What did it all mean? One thing was certain, they all seemed to think she was close, too close?

To see the big picture?

Sleep won the battle Naomi waged within her mind and that morning, she woke with Zelda curled beside her, to the darkness of the stairway and the frustration of missing clues, and the dawning realization that it was the first time in weeks she hadn't dreamt at all.

AN ACHING BACK now added to her worries, go figure, it turns out sleeping on the cold, hard floor of the stairwell wasn't the most comfortable way to sleep. Upon waking that morning, Naomi had searched for Bryce but discovered that his car was missing from the driveway. She checked her cell phone, but he hadn't called or texted. He had stated that he needed space, but she had to know if there was any new information regarding Holly.

As if he read her mind, a text beeped from her phone.

*Holly is okay. She's at my parents' house.*

She cried out loud, tears streaming down her face. It was okay. Holly was safe. Things could go back to normal, whatever their normal was.

*Thank God. Thank you for letting me know. Please call me when you can.*

She had to talk to him, find out the details of how they had found Holly. He didn't respond, but she could wait. Now that she knew Holly was safe, she could wait this part out.

Another text. This time it was Miriam.

*Heard the news. Holly is safe and sound.*

*Can I come over?*

*Sure. Coffee's on.*

Naomi could use a friend, and she could also use a cup of coffee. She hurried over to Miriam's place, noting how much cooler it was here than in Florida. Hard to believe that this time yesterday, she and Bryce were enjoying a romantic, relaxing getaway. She huffed as she admitted the truth to herself; looking back, there wasn't much relaxation or romance taking place by the end of their trip.

Whose car was this in Miriam's driveway? The red SUV looked vaguely familiar. She knocked on the door and waited for Miriam to greet her.

"Hey, is this not a good time?"

"No, come on in. I was just chatting with Cole." She paused. "About the case."

Cole smiled as he stood to shake her hand. "Hey, Naomi. Sorry to hear about all the trouble with Holly, but I'm so glad she's okay."

"Yeah, thanks."

Glancing around, Naomi noticed there were bagels and a crumb cake on the table. She moved Miriam's laptop computer to the side and settled in at the table.

"Hungry? Cole brought some breakfast over earlier."

She watched the way Miriam and Cole looked at one another, and she would put money on the fact that there was, indeed, chemistry brewing between them. She wondered to herself how much time they had spent together since she left town.

"No, I can't eat a thing right now. Tell me what you know about Holly."

"Didn't Bryce tell you?"

"Not exactly. He said she was okay."

"That's it?"

"We're not exactly on steady ground right now. He says he needs space."

"Space? What does that mean?"

Cole cleared his throat and excused himself to the bathroom. He was a smart man, she noted once more. What guy wants to get involved in a conversation with women about man troubles?

"Space. That's what he said. He needs time. I can't say I blame him, but now that Holly has been found, maybe he'll come around sooner."

"Yeah, you know he's been extremely patient with you, I don't know that most men would stick around for all this–"

"Drama?"

"Not the word I was looking for, but that works. You know what I mean. It was one thing when it was just you he needed to worry about, but now this Lillie girl is going after Holly."

Tell her something that she didn't know. "How *was* Holly found?"

"She woke up in her bed at her grandparents' house, claiming to have played with her friend whom she wouldn't name for a bit in the attic of your house and then she simply woke up in bed." The attic? The police had searched the attic and hadn't seen any signs of Holly.

"Friend?" She cringed although she had known it all along.

"The police are visiting every one of her friends' homes." Miriam whispered the information and Naomi couldn't blame her for not wanting Cole to overhear this insanity. "Naomi—I didn't say anything to my co-workers about Lillie. I mean, what would I say?"

"That my family is screwed?"

"Stop that."

"It's true. I begged Lillie last night, *begged* her to stop this nonsense."

"I don't think it's nonsense to her, though. Something really bad happened to her, and she's blaming you, unfortunately."

"Yeah, because she hates her own parents and has no one else to take it out on."

"Maybe."

"What are you getting at?"

"Oh, I don't know, Naomi. I suspect it's more than just displaced anger. She is *quite* angry, and she appears to not only take it out on you, but from where I sit, it's as if she *blames* you."

She pondered over Miriam's words and then recalled her recent dream in which Sharon Wilde had appeared and told her to look for the little things. She shifted gears.

"Hey, Miriam?"

"Yes?"

"Don't take this the wrong way, but I think there's something about the crime scene or Sharon's house that we overlooked."

"Overlooked?"

"Yes, I think so. I had a dream, and in my dream, Sharon actually told me to look for the little things."

"Okay, first of all, you know it wasn't Sharon. Scratch that–with you it could actually *be*, but what could we have missed?"

"I don't know, but I think we should go back and look at both the crime scene and her house, or maybe even the ex-husband's apartment."

"How do you suppose we do that? He's not an official suspect at this point, and we don't have a search warrant."

"Minor details. We'll have to figure it out."

"Says the writer. Listen, we can't just go walking into this guy's house on a feeling, a voice from a dream."

Cole cleared his throat, announcing his presence. "Listen, I didn't mean to eavesdrop, but since it is my sister you're talking about, I'm going to chime in here."

"Yes?" Miriam prompted.

"What do you say we question Barry's date a bit more? I have a nagging feeling we weren't asking all of the right questions." He stopped to shrug his shoulders. "Sorry, Miriam."

"No, I mean, this is your sister. I get it. What kind of questions do you think we should have asked her?"

Naomi had never seen someone question Miriam's thoroughness and walk away from it alive. Well, perhaps she was being a bit dramatic, but for Miriam to take it so well?

Suddenly, Naomi considered the words from her dream, and she glanced around the room. Little things. Little things. Naomi glanced around the table as she fiddled with her wedding ring. Little things. Little things.

"That's it!"

"What?" Miriam lifted her head.

"Does Barry still wear his wedding ring?"

"Yeah, the jackass refused to believe it was over, even at the end." Cole sighed.

"Your computer. Can I see it for a minute?"

"Yeah, sure."

"What was the name of that dating website you said Barry was on?"

"Coupled Hearts, why? We checked on her story. They went on one date, and she said although she liked him, he never called again. She said it was odd because she thought it went well and he seemed interested."

"Coupled Hearts, Coupled Hearts." Naomi spoke to herself as she perused the site. "Damn, I have to provide my email to search?"

"That's the way those sites work," Cole said and then looked down. "I mean that's what I–" He stopped, turning red in the face.

"It's okay, Cole. I can't say I've done it myself, but I don't judge," Miriam offered. Naomi marveled at the distinct talent Miriam had for both insulting someone and then putting them at ease, all at the same time.

"It's hard out there," Cole admitted.

"I know," Miriam said gently.

So it appeared that Cole *was* single.

Typing in her email address, Naomi searched male profiles in the area. No sign of Barry. "Did you guys actually see his profile up here?"

"No, he claims he took it down after the murder, saying it didn't feel right to have women contacting him after Sharon had been killed," Miriam stated.

"So we don't actually know that he was ever really on the site."

"His date that night claimed he was. She confirmed his alibi."

"So you don't believe me when I say I'm positive Barry killed her? With his own hands?"

Miriam sighed deeply. "I do believe that you're sure about that, and I'm not saying it isn't true. But I'm also looking at the facts here. I've been wondering if sometimes your visions, feelings, might sometimes become mixed with your own thoughts, your own suspicions."

She couldn't listen to Miriam's doubts right now.

An idea sprang to life. "Can we call this woman?"

"We spoke with her already, but sure, we could call her again. What are you thinking?"

"Bear with me here. I want to confirm the fact that the man she went on a date with was actually Barry."

"Who else would it have been?" Miriam responded.

"That's what I'm trying to figure out. Listen, if you were on a date with a man, and he either *still* had his ring on, or just as bad, had the telltale marks on his finger of a man who had *just* removed his ring, would you be gung ho to date him again? *And* would you fail to mention that to the police?"

"I–hadn't thought that through."

"She's right, Miriam, she might be on to something." Cole pointed his finger at Naomi, nodding his head.

"Thanks Cole. Now help me out here. Call her up, and ask her to meet us."

Miriam reluctantly picked up her cell and made the call.

# CHAPTER FOURTEEN

WHILE THEY WAITED to speak with the woman from the dating site, who was named Cindy, later that afternoon, she and Miriam had headed back to the house and then to the facility with Cole to see if there was anything else they had overlooked.

"I don't think we missed anything here," Miriam said for what had to be the hundredth time.

Naomi didn't either, but that didn't stop her from opening her mind to the possibility. Instead of focusing on solving Sharon's murder though, she had inadvertently opened up the floodgates to Lillie.

There she was, invading her mind, the little urchin. Lillie now sat in this very room, for Naomi recognized it from the fireplace, but once more, the room was clean. Clean, yes, but the noxious odor of urine and other uncleanly stenches nearly made her vomit. Naomi often picked up on smells within her visions, so this was no surprise.

Lillie rocked gently in an antique rocking chair–back and forth, back and forth. Today, she didn't cry but rather appeared pensive, deep in thought. A nurse walked in and handed her some medication and a glass of water to wash it down. Lillie gulped back the water and waited until the nurse left the room. Naomi watched closely, for as soon as the door closed shut and the nurse was out of sight, Lillie spit the pills out from under her tongue into her hand and ran to the bathroom where she flushed them down the small toilet. She walked over to her dresser and grabbed her doll, taking it with her to sit back down on the rocking chair. The door opened again and an older man appeared this time, rattling off question after question. It seemed Lillie had become an expert of sorts when it came to answering them. Naomi watched in awe as the smart little girl followed out her designed plan.

*"How are you feeling today?"*

*"Good, Dr. Berton, much better today."*

*"I'm glad to hear it. Now, have you given any thought to our talk yesterday?"*

*"Yes, I have. I think you're right. I believe it was my imagination."*

*"So you agree that there were no slaves, no family, at your house? That this family is what we might refer to as imagined friends, conjured up out of boredom perhaps?"*

*"Yes, Doctor."*

*"And you no longer wish to run from here and save them from being killed, now do you?"* The doctor leaned over, speaking very softly. Lillie didn't so much as flinch when she responded perfectly to his questions.

*"That would be silly. They don't exist."*

"*Very good, then. Of course they don't. Seems you're on your way to recovery.*"

*Lillie smiled.* "*So can I go back home now?*" *The hope in her eyes broke Naomi's heart, for she feared the girl wouldn't ever go home to a normal family again.*

"*No, young lady,*" *the doctor replied swiftly, shaking his head.* "*It's too soon, far too soon. You see, it's only through a combination of medication and talking this over that you ever will truly be well. It will take time, and I've advised your parents to let you remain here for a while, just so we can be sure.*"

*Disappointment and fear shot through Lillie's features, she clenched her hands tightly and stood, she then composed herself, took a moment to relax, and sat back down again.*

"*That was much better, much better than last time, Lillian. You don't want us to have to put you in the other room for getting too excited again. He drew a syringe out of his coat jacket and fiddled with the top.* "*Here, this will help.*"

"*I took my medicine. I don't need anymore. I just want my mother. I want to see my mother, I want to see Duchess!*" *Lillie was smart, but she was also a little girl. And she had been human, crying out for her mother again had earned her a quick jab of the needle in her arm.*

"*I told your mother and father it would be best if they stayed away for this first part of the treatment. I think it's easier on all of you this way.*"

*As Lillie became groggy from her medication, Naomi cried as she watched the little girl's eyelids grow heavy, giving in to her drug-induced slumber. She didn't understand what happened next—why a teenage boy stuck his head in the room while the doctor administered the shot and why his gaze lingered on Lillie.*

*What could it mean? It had to be important, but why? Confusion set in, and the more sense she tried to make out of what she just saw, the less she knew. Right now, she couldn't think at all. Her head throbbed, preventing her from doing anything but cry out.*

One arm steadied her on each side as Naomi came out of her trance. She looked up to see the faces of Miriam and Cole.

"What happened? What did you see?" Miriam barked the questions out, but Naomi needed time to stop the pounding in her head. Feeling the thunderous emotions of Lillie sapped the life out of her, and she needed a minute to recover.

"I—it's not about Sharon. It was Lillie."

Miriam shot her a confused glance. "Again? Why the hell do thoughts of her keep popping up whenever we're here?"

Now she knew. It had taken a while, and she should have figured it out earlier, but now she knew. "It's because this is where her parents sent her. They sent her away—to this mental hospital." And it also explained why she hated her mother and father so much.

My God—pieces clicked together, snap—snap—snapping into place. Lillie had shared the same gift, or sometimes curse, that Naomi had—as a child, she had had the ability to see ghosts, to speak with them. She must have thought she could save the slaves, didn't understand they were already dead. She would have gone to her parents for help. She must have told them what she saw. The parents had sent her away. Way back then, there was little knowledge of effective psychotherapy. Most issues were tended to with drugs, and many people went to asylums to be treated—asylums from which many would never return.

Oh, Lillie, I'm so sorry. What happened to you?

O<small>F ALL THE</small> things that had happened today, her mind still went to Bryce and all of their troubles. Still no word from him. It had been hours since she had texted him last, telling him that she needed to speak with him, that she missed him. She wanted to share what she had learned about Lillie but then considered that he wouldn't want to hear it. What would she do if he refused to speak with her? Shut her out? She didn't think she could handle that right now, or ever.

"There she is." Miriam nodded at the door to the coffee shop where they had come for a chance to regroup after leaving the mental hospital, and Naomi got her mind back to the business at hand. Along with the worries on her mind, thoughts of Ryan surfaced as well since this café used to be their favorite meeting spot when they were searching out clues about Maggie's death.

"Hi, Cindy. Thank you for meeting with us again." Miriam shook Cindy's hand, and she and Cole did the same.

"What can I do for you?" Cindy's brown eyes made contact with each of them. She smoothed her blouse and waited for them to speak.

"This is Naomi, a good friend of mine and also somewhat of a communicator with spirits."

Naomi waited for the usual look of skepticism she often encountered when people first heard this, but instead, she found that Cindy didn't so much as flinch.

"Do you mind if I ask you some questions, Cindy?"

"No, of course not. I have great appreciation for what you do. One of my aunts had the ability to interact with ghosts. I kind of hoped I had the same talent, but no—nothing here." Cindy smiled nervously, throwing up her hands with a slight giggle.

"Did you ever actually see a photograph of Barry?"

"Yes, his profile photo, of course."

"Here." Miriam handed a photograph of Barry to Cindy. "Is this the man you went on a date with?"

Cindy's smile froze, then her mouth turned down to a frown. "No, that's not right. That's not him." She curled her lip and searched for answers on their faces.

She *knew it.* Miriam's composure broke as she pointed to the photograph. "Look closely, Cindy, please." She jabbed her finger right in the center of the photo.

"I am. It's not him, although honestly, they could pass as brothers. My date had all the same coloring—dark hair, brown eyes, same hairstyle. My date was tall, maybe six foot one?"

Miriam cursed aloud and didn't seem to care about the stares she drew from the customers seated at the table behind them. "By all accounts, they share the same characteristics. What did he do? Hire someone to pretend to be him?"

"And that would explain why he never called!" Cindy cried out, slapping her leg. She smiled widely and then realized the inappropriateness of her behavior. "I'm sorry, that was wrong, very wrong." She turned her face down and gazed at the floor.

"No worries. I would have been pissed that he hadn't called as well." Naomi lightened the mood and winked at Cindy, who visibly relaxed her shoulders. "At least that's one mystery solved, right?"

"Right," Cindy stated, keeping a lid on her exuberance.

"So now you get to tell us every word he said, no matter

how irrelevant it may seem." Miriam whipped out her note pad and jotted down everything Cindy brought to the table.

Her mind should have been on the case, but instead, it teetered between Bryce, Holly, and Lillie. Now that she knew why Lillie was so pissed, what could she do about it? And how had Lillie died? That piece of Lillie's little puzzle was still missing. She checked her cell and pouted at the absence of any word from Bryce. When she couldn't stand it another second, Naomi grabbed her jacket and excused herself for a moment and decided to try to call Bryce in private.

Stepping outside into the brisk air, Naomi tightened her jacket around her and made the call. He picked up after several rings.

"Bryce."

"Yeah, I was going to call you when things settled down here."

"How is she? How's Holly?"

The brief pause caused her stomach to flip. "She's frightened but still loyal to Lillie, and well, she'll be okay."

"Thank God. I don't even know what to say to you. It's my fault, and I don't know how to make this better."

Another pause, and then he sighed. "Neither do I. This is probably the hardest thing I'll ever have to do, Naomi." His voice wobbled with emotion. Fear washed through her as she steeled herself for his next words.

"Bryce—"

"Naomi, listen. Dammit, listen for once." He stopped for a moment before continuing, "I have thought this through, every *single* angle, every *single* possibility, and my gut is telling me that I need to protect my daughter."

"From me?" She could barely say the words.

"Not from you, no, but *because* of you."

She couldn't speak. She couldn't breathe.

"I love you more than life itself, but you have to understand. I also love my daughter with all my heart, and she's seven years old, Naomi, *seven*. I need to get her out of that house, away from all of this, before the next time, when it doesn't end with Holly back in my arms."

She sobbed, nodding her understanding yet hating the words pouring from his mouth. She didn't try to stop the endless stream of tears running down her face. She grasped at straws, saying anything to change his mind. "I–I know more about her, I'm so cl–close to figuring this out, figuring *her* out. Just give me some time," she stammered over her words as her body quaked.

"I'm so, so sorry, sweetheart. I wish there was another way. I'm going to miss you so much, more than you can imagine. But I need to be strong, and I need you to let me be. Don't try to change my mind. Can you do that for me?" His voice rose in despair.

She nodded silently, tears covering her neck as she paced the area behind the restaurant, barely noticing the look on the face of one of the workers emptying the garbage into the dumpster.

"This is what we need to do. I'm in the process of packing some bags right now. Holly and I will stay with my parents." She placed a hand over her chest as she heard him cry out his own tears.

"Bryce–"

But he just continued on in his broken words, "You–I know eventually you'll figure this out. I need you to be careful since I can't be here to protect you–"

She couldn't stand the sound of his sobs anymore. It was way too much. "There has to be a way to make this work. I'm your wife, Bryce, your *wife*."

"I can't be here, so you'll need to protect yourself. When the dust finally settles, we'll reevaluate everything, but Naomi—"

"What is it, Bryce? What is it?" She nearly screamed the words.

"You remember what I said before? About you and who you attract? If this keeps happening, it's not going—"

"To work? Is that what you mean? Because, oh, let me see if I remember your exact words, "Who will it be next time? Jack the Ripper?"" Now she saw red, she understood he was protecting Holly, but she was *her* daughter, too. Wasn't that what their marriage was all about?

"I asked you not to do this. It's hard enough. Don't you think this is killing me?" he cried out, catching his breath. "I can't talk anymore."

"No, you don't. Oh no, you don't, Bryce. Now it's your turn to listen. You and I took a vow—for better or worse. We have a family together. This thing with Lillie? She's going to be stopped. I *will* stop her, and then it will be better, it'll be over. You can't just assume it will never stop. You can't just give up on me!"

"I'm not—"

"Not yet? Is that what you meant to say?"

His silence gave her the answer—the words he couldn't speak. She disconnected their call and threw her phone into the woods.

She had no idea how long she had been sitting alone on the grass near the dumpster, but when she glanced around, there stood Miriam and Cole, their eyes open wide.

"Give me a minute, Cole?" Miriam handed him the keys to her car and waited until he was seated in the passenger seat to approach Naomi.

"Sweetie, what happened?" She retrieved Naomi's cell phone and wiped the dirt from it before taking a seat down on the grass beside her. Miriam reached for her hand and then rocked a sobbing Naomi in her arms. Naomi cried out the words she thought she would never have to speak, the words that meant Bryce had finally, after everything they had been through, reached his breaking point.

# CHAPTER FIFTEEN

TRUE TO HIS word, Bryce had packed his bags and Holly's as well. She walked the bottom floor of the house for the third time and finally found herself in the kitchen, pouring herself a glass of red wine. Bryce loved this brand of wine and should be here drinking it alongside her, she thought. Taking a seat on the sofa, she twirled her hair, thinking she would go insane from missing Bryce and Holly. She took a longer sip of wine and then spied a piece of paper out of the corner of her eye. Naomi recognized Bryce's handwriting immediately. She gulped back yet another sip and read:

> *Naomi,*
> *I can't believe I'm sitting here writing a note*
> *I never in a million years thought I would have*
> *to write. You see, you're my wife, my life. Hav-*

*ing to take a break from you for just a while or forever is something neither of us can predict right now, for time and only time will tell us the answer to that question. I can promise you this; I will never find a better friend, lover, and mother for my child. Your empathy, your caring for others is also your downfall, I suppose. What drew me to you was your fierce loyalty and passion that you give to your loved ones, your writing, and everything you do. My heart is ripped in half, and the other side is with you, will always be with you, even if I can't. Don't try to figure this out right now, for I can't even begin to. Be strong, be brave, and maybe someday soon we can be together again, but baby, if we can't, I need you to hang on to that strength and give me some because I will be heartbroken. I'll always love you, but unfortunately, I'm learning the hard lesson that, sometimes in this world, we need more than love. Sometimes we need an answer to a prayer. Sometimes we need a miracle.*

*Forever yours,*

*Bryce*

She clutched the tear-stained letter to her chest, heaving endless sobs, both cursing him and loving him at the same time. Would she do the same if she were him? She figured right now, after what had happened with Holly, the answer would be yes.

What they needed was what Bryce spoke of—they needed a miracle.

Dᴿᴇᴀᴍs ᴏꜰ Bʀʏᴄᴇ, their wedding day, all of their happy times, fell flat when she woke and immediately remembered her reality. A cold, heard reality that sucked. She couldn't just lie in bed and wallow in her misery, though, and as much as she wanted to fight for him, she had to heed his wishes and leave him alone—for now, at least. The only thing she could do was to pursue Lillie and end this mess for good.

Naomi considered writing and felt a twinge of guilt that she had neglected her career lately, but she couldn't possibly write until she cleared her mind and settled her problems. At least this book wasn't on any deadlines since it was to be self-published.

A thought popped into her mind, and she knew it was exactly what she needed right now—good old-fashioned work. Heading up the stairs, she tried not to think of how lonely this big old house was now, just her and Zelda. Making her way to the guest room, she pulled the door to the attic open and walked up the dark stairs. She had only been up there once before since moving here, this part of the house wasn't connected with the secret passages, and she remembered how cluttered the back section was. Bryce had claimed that the previous owner, his friend, John, had left some stuff up there that had been sitting for many generations, from previous owners. Bryce hadn't wanted to break the tradition, so he had left the items alone. He had simply placed the piles in their own corner, stating they had more than enough room to share. Naomi had to agree and couldn't believe she had forgotten about the items.

She busied herself, tearing through the boxes one at a time, only pausing to swipe the dust from her eyes. When she heard the cries from Zelda as the cat approached the stairs, she had to smile. She and Zelda had some time to make up for, and she figured going through old boxes together, searching for clues, was a good start.

"Come here, you crazy cat." Zelda rubbed against Naomi as if she hadn't been behaving like a little traitor. "That's okay. I forgive you. How could I hold a grudge against you?" She leaned over and kissed a purring Zelda.

As she opened the next to last box in the stack, she hoped that she would find something tangible to the case. She reached her hand in and was met with resistance.

What the?

"Lesson number six." Lillie's bold voice shook the attic walls, and the box slammed shut around her fingers.

"Ouch."

Another box flew from a dark corner of the attic, this one containing pictures of Naomi. One particular photo showed her holding Zelda when she had first found her. In the photograph, a beaming Naomi held the cat to her face and kissed her.

"Lesson number six: don't take things that don't belong to you." Before Naomi could react, the photograph crumbled to pieces before her eyes, reduced to mere dust.

So Lillie was jealous.

Jealous of her relationship with Zelda. The cat mewed loudly and ran to a spot of the attic where Lillie now appeared. She stroked the cat, showing her pleasure that

Zelda had once again chosen her over Naomi.

"This isn't a popularity contest, Lillie. Zelda has room in her heart for both of us. I don't mind sharing."

"Well, I do. I don't like to share with others." Of course, it didn't surprise her that the childish side of Lillie now spoke. Naomi supposed it was a lesson Lillie had never had the chance to learn.

She rubbed at her hand, wincing. "You speak of lessons, Lillie? Well, here's one for you. *You* should learn to share. You'd be surprised how happy it can make you."

Another box rushed forward, this one making contact with the top of her head. "Lillie, that's enough!" She rubbed her head and felt disappointment that Zelda hadn't even reacted, hadn't come to her rescue.

"Lesson number seven: don't you *ever, ever* even think of teaching me a lesson." An antique lamp hovered, slamming into her face. Naomi swept her hair out of eyes, wincing in pain. How many lessons were there? She was afraid to ask.

"Okay, okay. Lillie, enough. I saw what you went through at the hospital. How can I help you?"

Every window shook with the rage of a madwoman—make that a mad child. She heard the distinct cracking of glass and covered her face as shards of glass flew inches from her head. Finally, she heard the cries from Zelda and then the feral hiss of a really pissed off cat. So, Zelda did have her back when it came down to it.

"Lesson number eight: mind your own damn business!" The wind that had entered the room from the attic windows swirled and whipped around her, the pieces of glass slicing into her skin. But she knew better than to remove her hands from her face. So she sat powerless until Zelda's cries drew near, and only when the cat came closer to Naomi did the madness end.

"You don't fight fair, little girl." Naomi didn't have the strength to hide her tears. She was past the point of trying. Blood seeped from her hands as she picked the glass and its splinters from her arms and hands. "You're more powerful than me. I don't have any superpowers, so what do you want from me? Do you want to kill me? Don't torture me then. Why don't you just get it over with?" She wasn't stopping. Her rant continued, and it felt good and she wasn't prepared to quit, not now.

"You ruined my marriage, ruined my family! You've made me miserable. You've taken my cat from me. Tell me, you little, rotten child–what the hell do you want from me?"

She shook with a rage of her own, one that didn't shatter windows or conjure up the storm of the century, but she did feel its power, and it gave her the courage to speak her mind and stomp after Lillie.

Lillie appeared, disappeared then reappeared again all over the attic. She couldn't catch the girl but realized she couldn't do much even if she was able to get close to her. Just as Naomi prepared to turn around and leave this scene and Lillie's drama behind her, she saw it.

The black and white tattered photograph had seen better days, but what she saw was unmistakable. Her blood-stained hands shook as she reached down to grab the photo of a smiling little blonde haired girl and her black cat.

"Holy–"

She sank to the floor, her eyes seeking out Lillie and Zelda across the room. Lillie held the cat possessively, and Naomi saw tears streaming down her little face.

Lillie and Zelda–preserved for all time in black and white, right before her eyes. There was no mistaking Zelda;

she would know her cat anywhere. The single tiny dot of gray that dotted the underside of her chin stood out like a beacon in the photograph, her familiar eyes piercing into Naomi, even in the aged photo.

"Don't worry, Lillie," she gently whispered. "I won't take your cat away from you. Duchess belongs with you." Naomi couldn't be sure, but she would have sworn Lillie's features had softened just a bit.

# CHAPTER SIXTEEN

How in the world was it possible that the cat in the photograph, dating back to what must be over a hundred years, was indeed Zelda? It was beyond Naomi. It went far beyond her realm of comprehension.

But in her bones, in her heart, she knew, without a doubt, that it was Zelda, for she knew her cat to the core. And if that was a fact, then how was it possible that this ghost of a cat had eluded her all these years? Kept this phenomenal, supernatural secret? The cat had duped not only her, but her friends and family as well. *Everyone* seemed to have the ability to see Zelda.

She expelled a bitter laugh as she imagined Bryce's reaction if she shared this tidbit of information with him right now. No, probably not the best time to break the news.

No wonder Zelda had hit it off so splendidly with Maggie, *no wonder.* The spirit of Maggie and the cat had a lot in common it appeared. Part of her understood the childish display of jealousy on Lillie's part when it came to Zelda, for now she, too, felt a bitter stab of envy. Zelda didn't belong to her. In reality, she had *never* belonged to Naomi, and that admission stung. It had to be tough, though, for Lillie and Zelda to have been apart for all these years. Had they somehow lost each other, perhaps in an intricate maze in the alternate universe they resided in?

But Naomi found herself smiling because it had been due to her that Zelda and Lillie had crossed paths, had found one another after all these years. At least, there was one small benefit of this disaster. She considered the strong bond Lillie and Zelda shared and had to admit it felt good to help reunite what appeared to be the best of friends. Maybe Lillie would even lighten up a bit on her. One could only hope.

Now that a new day was upon her, Naomi grabbed a cup of coffee from the kitchen and checked her phone for what must have been the twentieth time since she had woken. More texts from Miriam showed up on her screen but nothing from Bryce. It took a tremendous amount of willpower on her part not to call him, but she practiced restraint and instead thought of him nearly every waking moment since their separation two days earlier.

*Keep busy,* she told herself. It was becoming her new mantra. *Stay busy, and solve Lillie's problems...your problems.* It was all she could do, the only thing to stop her from driving herself mad, for right now, she had little control of anything else.

"Lillie? Where are you?" But the pint-sized hellion refused to show her face since their interaction in the attic, and Zelda, for that matter, had disappeared as well.

Glancing at the clock on the kitchen wall, Naomi knew

she didn't have a lot of time before she had to meet up with Miriam and Cole. Miriam had texted her that they had some new information about the case she wanted to share with her. Normally, she would have been at Miriam's door in a heartbeat, but today she had more pressing matters to attend to first.

There had to be some reason Lillie's soul seemed to glue itself to her, first as a child, now all these years later. And for lack of other options, Naomi decided it was high time to tackle something she had always wanted to do but had never taken the time to before, since nothing else up in the attic was helpful besides the photograph, and she didn't have much to go on there.

With a faint grin on her face, Naomi powered up her computer and typed in the names of one of the ancestry websites she had always been curious about. No better time than the present, she mused as her fingers tapped away at the keyboard. What if there was some connection here that she was missing? To her or to this house?

The most basic functions of the site were free, but Naomi knew the bare bones wouldn't work in this case and that this wasn't the time to be frugal. "Ah, what the hell," Naomi said aloud as she reached over the table for her bag and pulled out her debit card.

"What is this?" Naomi felt like a child in a candy shop as she took in all of the available information she could gain by accessing her family tree. But she knew in order to gain the most useful, comprehensive information, she would have to submit a swab of saliva for her DNA. Shoot—that would take weeks, but what choice did she have? When she finished ordering the kit, she veered back to the family tree section of the website and spent some more money on the middle-grade package, which allowed her to search data outside of the United States.

Frustration piled high as Naomi soon discovered that without a photograph of Lillie on this site, how the heck would she find anything on her? But wait–she did know the surnames of the previous owners–yes, so therefore, she could research the family, without the saliva swab, of course.

So many names, so much information to sort through. When it came to researching ghosts, this was the first time she was working solo. Ryan had helped her with Maggie, and of course Bryce had played a significant part in researching both Maggie and Nick's deaths. *Suck it up,* she told herself. *Suck it up and get to work.*

She stood to stretch and grab a pad of paper and a pen, then she took the better part of an hour to jot down notes on her findings. Besides learning that the surnames Bailey, Johnson, Hall, and Alexander were as popular as they came in the late 1800's through the early 1900's, Naomi couldn't discover much more for the moment. She had to get to Miriam's house soon, and her head pounded with a host of unanswered questions. Lillie's time of birth proved difficult to pin down as her clothing in both ghostly form and the photograph could cover the span of many years.

"Until later, Lillie," she called out. "You know it would be a hell of a lot easier if you simply told me your last name and when you lived here," she added.

No answer. Of course not, not when she needed something from her, she mused once more.

Grabbing her jacket from the hook near the front door, she frowned when she noted the absence of Holly and Bryce's jackets. She shook her head and marched outside, spying the red SUV from here. She grinned, ever so slightly. Cole was becoming a regular fixture over at Miriam's place.

Before she had the chance to knock on Miriam's door, it flew open. "Come on, we've been waiting for you!" Miriam pulled her hand and swept her inside.

"Whoa. Way too early in the day for this energy, Miriam. Take it down a notch."

"Zip it. Sit down, and listen. Cole, you're on coffee duty," she ordered as she pointed at the coffee pot.

"Yes, ma'am," Cole responded, dutifully grabbing a mug for Naomi. He poured the coffee and placed it before her.

"I could have done that," she offered, noticing that Cole sipped his coffee from Naomi's favorite mug. He was becoming very comfortable here, but as she gazed at Miriam's beaming grin, she liked what she saw. She glanced at Miriam, who swiped her hand across the space in front of her, dismissing Naomi. Miriam could be proud, and at times, her stubbornness proved to be her own worst enemy; hopefully it wouldn't affect her possibly blooming romantic relationship.

"What's up?"

"We found him."

"Who?"

"The guy that Barry *paid* to pretend to be him."

"What?"

"Yes, Barry's misstep was not making sure the fool took his profile down. We searched the local men, zeroing in on his age range, and boom–there he was."

"But we searched for the name Barry–"

"No, he went by a nickname, B.J. Can you believe it? Everything else checked out, from his coloring to his eyes to his height."

"Wow." She digested the information. "So that's it? It's

a wrap?"

"Not quite. Now we get the search order for his apartment, and when we do, I suspect everything else will fall into place."

"And B.J.?"

"B.J. was offered money in exchange for a little role-playing. Not the highest morals around, but I get the feeling he's just a guy who didn't think through some rather stupid actions–can't arrest a guy for that."

"Right. Who knows? Maybe he figured Barry was a married guy out there playing some strange head games," Cole interjected. "The important thing is that we got that son of a bitch–we finally got Barry right where we need him."

"Not yet, Cowboy, but soon." Miriam winked at Cole, who smiled back, blushing slightly.

Was this how she and Bryce had appeared to others in the beginning? How had everything gone so bad, so quickly? She would give anything to have him by her side right now, to hold him again. She realized Miriam was speaking and she hadn't heard a word she had said.

"Well? Are you ready to go?"

Naomi spun her head in Miriam's direction. "Where are we going?"

"*We're* not going anywhere. Cole and I are heading out to breakfast. To discuss the case, of course," Miriam added with a nod of her head.

"Oh."

"See you later." Miriam grabbed her jacket, leading the way outside. Naomi nodded her head in approval as she followed Miriam and Cole out the door.

Later that week, three things happened. First, Bryce had texted her, claiming that he missed her, but he couldn't talk to her. Not yet. She'd take it.

Next, she had received her expedited DNA kit in the mail and had promptly supplied a saliva sample and mailed the package back with crossed fingers that the results would produce something worthwhile.

Finally, Lillie had materialized and hadn't harmed Naomi but rather watched her, with Zelda curled in her tiny arms. Had it been the fact that Zelda had stuck up for Naomi back there in the attic that had caused this small miracle, or was it the simple, yet profound words that Naomi had recently spoke?

*I won't take your cat away from you.*

Maybe it had been the combination, but whatever the reason, she was grateful. If only she could get Lillie to answer some questions, then she would be home free.

The old expression "You can't always get what you want" rang through her mind, and she told herself to be thankful for small favors. She could really do without the lumps and bruises Lillie had loved to hash out to her.

And just when Naomi thought she had about all the excitement she could handle for the week, another thing happened. Miriam had arrested Barry, and he was currently in jail with a bail set so high he couldn't possibly spring free. Miriam had found the pair of gloves, which Naomi had seen in her vision with Sharon's DNA all over them. Barry's DNA had also matched the samples retrieved from the crime scene.

Naomi had nearly forgotten one more positive thing: she had seen Cole's SUV in Miriam's driveway nearly every night this week, which confirmed her suspicions that the two would keep in touch after the case was settled.

She kept waiting for one more good thing to happen, one where Bryce would call her up and tell her how foolish he had been and that he couldn't wait to see her. But he hadn't been unwise, rather he had been smart to stay away. She could tell him that Lillie had changed, no devilish pranks since the night she had relinquished her rights to Zelda. But yeah, she still hung around, actually more now, following Naomi, staring at her, watching her without uttering a word. At times, her silence was nearly as disconcerting as her rage had been, only because Naomi had no idea what was on Lillie's mind now.

A rapping sound at her front door startled her, and she nearly spilled the wine she had been holding all over her blouse. Padding her way to the door, Naomi peered through the peephole and sucked in her breath at the sight of Bryce on the other side of the door.

Before she got too carried away, she tamped down her grin, silently warning herself not to get too excited. There could be a multitude of reasons for this visit.

"Bryce." She opened the screen door, taking in his sleep deprived, sunken eyes. She frowned and had to stop herself from reaching out to touch him.

"Hi, I—I'm here to pick up some more of Holly's pajamas and a few other things."

"Oh." Disappointment washed over her. "Of course, come in." She opened the door wide and stepped back. He appeared thinner, older somehow. Did she look the same to him? She hadn't bothered to glance at her reflection in the mirror for more than the few seconds it took to brush her hair and throw some light makeup on.

"Naomi—I—" But he shook his head when he made eye contact then sucked in a breath and darted up the stairs toward Holly's room. So it hurt him to see her. That had to mean something. She sucked in Bryce's pain as if it were her own, which of course, it was.

*It hurts me, too.*

He had no idea how much it did. It felt as if her heart had been ripped out of her chest. She gave him the space he had requested and tried to busy herself with a chore so that she wasn't just standing there like an ass when he came back downstairs.

"I'm leaving now."

Oh. She had been so deep in thought as she stood in the kitchen, rewashing dishes that had already been sparkling clean. She hadn't heard his approaching footsteps. She turned to face him, and they stood silent, for just a second, staring at each other as if answers would miraculously appear before them.

"Okay." She turned off the faucet and then wiped her hands on her jeans. A hand went to her hair, twisting the strands around her fingers as she tried to peel her gaze from his face.

"Stop that." He touched her fingers, causing them to still. Her heart stopped as she prayed he would say something, anything to her.

Anything to get him to stay.

For a moment, his eyes softened, and he leaned in closer, ever so slightly. "I have to go." And the moment was gone. She followed him to the doorway, and she suddenly *knew.* As if reading his mind, she *knew.* He had already made his decision; she had seen it in his eyes, felt it in her soul. Unless this continual madness of seeing ghosts and solving their troubles came to an end, *their* troubles wouldn't cease. He couldn't do this—as much as he loved her, he needed to protect Holly from her.

He left her standing there, first staring at his retreating form, then the door he had shut behind him.

# CHAPTER SEVENTEEN

Weeks later, the torment, her own little piece of hell, continued. Bryce had stopped by a few times, texted a couple of times, but nothing had changed. She hated to see the pain and anguish on his face, the shadows that now seemed to reside permanently under his eyes. If she could make it stop, she would, in a heartbeat, because Bryce and Holly were her world.

She turned at the feel of a chill in the air and watched as Lillie appeared before her in the den. Lillie twirled a strand of her hair, around and around her little finger, just like Naomi had done so many times. A purring Zelda curled up beside Lillie on the small couch across the room, but the cat had her eyes on Naomi. Was Lillie copying her with this habit of playing with her hair? She couldn't tell what Lillie had on her mind anymore.

"Lillie." She stood, pushing her chair out from her desk.

Each time the duo appeared, Naomi attempted to speak with Lillie but didn't dare approach Zelda. Neither Lillie nor Zelda made a move. The creepy, precarious stares from both child and cat irked Naomi, to say it was unsettling was an understatement.

"Guys, I'm here when you want to talk," she attempted once more but shook her head when the two disappeared into thin air.

"Great, just freaking great. Again, my life is on hold because nobody will make a move. No one is helping me here." Naomi knew her complaint would be for naught, but she had to speak because the damn silence in this home was downright deafening.

Naomi sat back down at her desk and checked her email for the zillionth time this week. The results from the ancestry site had to be ready soon, she thought. Upon checking her email, she nearly jumped out of her chair. This was the first thing all week that had given her any hope of moving on from this dreadful situation.

"Come on," she muttered as she scanned the information then went back and studied the data with more attention.

"What are you looking for?" Lillie materialized before her eyes, sitting atop her desk, Zelda in her arms.

"My God—you frightened me." It was the closest Lillie had ever physically been to her, with the exception of the times she had physically harmed her, and Naomi wondered if it could mean something.

"What you're looking for, Naomi, has been right in front of your face this whole time. You're too close to see it, though, too jaded by the details of human life to open your mind to what you should have figured out long ago. Shame on you. Shame on you, Naomi. You've lost a lot because of your naivety."

The little girl now spoke with the precision and wisdom of a much older soul, which of course, she was. Her message was so similar to those of the ghosts of Augusta. They had all tried to tell her the same thing in, unfortunately, the same frustrating way.

"Can't you tell me, then? Why not just *tell me what you want.*"

"Oh, no. This is something you need to figure out on your own. You're closer, but this is a lesson you must work through."

"A lesson?" She had thought those cryptic lessons were over.

"Lesson number nine: open your eyes and stop being so damn stubborn!" The ghost and her cat vanished, leaving Naomi with a stark vision of the hidden passageway, complete with the family that had lost their lives. She watched again as the men approached, raised their rifles, and took aim, ending the lives of all the family members in mere seconds.

"Stop it, Lillie." Naomi winced, grabbing at her throbbing temples. "I've seen it all. What *aren't* you telling me?"

Open your eyes.

Open your eyes.

What was she talking about? *How* was she too close to the situation? What could that even mean?

She knew the stress was getting to her as the pounding echoes of her head hurt more and more with each day.

Naomi took a moment to rub her head and then went to the freezer and placed some ice cubes in a plastic baggie. She wrapped a paper towel around the bag and placed it to her head before grabbing some water.

"You're killing me, Lillie, killing me," she whined aloud

as she padded back to the den.

Once seated back at her desk, Naomi continued to review the results of her ancestry swab. After spending too much time reviewing her initial results showing that she was, indeed, of mostly Irish descent, she prodded further, finally stumbling upon what she had been looking for all along.

"Alexander," she whispered as a faint prickle waltzed across the length of her arms. "Alexander...Bailey" She grabbed the printout of her family tree and swiped her finger across the web of surnames. She stopped here and there as she made her way from her name to the names of many ancestors past.

"There!" She stabbed her finger on the spot of the tree that finally gave her something to go on.

An intricate path led her exactly where she needed to be. "Bailey."

"Bailey." Bailey had been one of the surnames that tied itself to her own. A flash of the woman who had stood baking with Lillie in a past vision drew closer, clearer, causing the aching in her head to worsen.

Dark brown hair, brown eyes, the slope of her nose, curve of her mouth...

"Holy–"

Naomi slammed the laptop shut and stood with wobbling knees, gasping for air that proved hard to find. She steadied her hand on the side of her desk and closed her eyes, trying to ease the incessant booming in her head, booming that made it difficult to stand.

Slumping to the floor, her legs gave way, and she sat, hugging her knees to her chest as she cried out to Lillie. Now she *knew*; now she *saw*. The woman, Lillie's *mother* had been the spitting image of Naomi, save for the old-fashioned clothing and style of hair.

"Lillie. Lillie, come here." Her voice shook as she called for the girl to surface.

My God—she should have seen it, should have *known…* Not only did she and Lillie share the same ability to see and interact with ghosts, but they shared more—so much more.

She and Lillie were family.

FOR ONCE, NAOMI could start to see the big picture, or at least the beginnings of it. *Why* Lillie had sought her out was no longer a mystery. *Why* she had been drawn here, to this house, was also clear. What part had meeting Bryce played? Had she been destined to meet him, fated to marry him and, therefore, raise their family in the home in which Lillie had lived? She believed so.

Instead of being freaked out about her ties to Bryce, she felt the opposite. She felt closer to Bryce than ever. She needn't have questioned whether she and Bryce were fated to be together, but it was kind of nice *knowing* the path she had taken with him had been meant to be all along. So would it be a cruel twist of fate if he were taken from her now?

She wouldn't allow herself to believe that was the course meant for them, wouldn't even consider the possibility.

So now what? What could she do to help Lillie? Although she knew most of what had drawn Lillie to her, she had some unanswered questions. For one, why all the anger on Lillie's part? She suspected the anger was due to the fact that Naomi bore such a striking resemblance to Lillie's mother, and that she was the only living relative within reach that Lillie could take out all of her rage and emotions regarding her treatment at the mental facility and then her subsequent death.

How had she died? That was the other looming question that needed to be answered.

Also, the lessons. All of the cruel, twisted lessons that Lillie had enjoyed dishing out. Had those been her own harsh childhood lessons? It made her wonder.

First things first, she had to uncover the cause of death. Her obituary had been discovered within the information, cause of death was vague, too vague for Naomi's taste: Undetermined sickness/malaise.

Malaise? Come on, hadn't anyone questioned such a thing? Had her parents tried covering something up? But what?

The staircase. Her gut screamed that whatever had occurred must have taken place in that stairway. But it didn't make sense that she would have even been able to find her way back to this home if she were still an inpatient of the facility.

Reaching for her bag, Naomi sprinted to the door and headed for the place that she hoped would start the unraveling of questions to a mystery that dated back so long ago, one that Naomi should have had resolved long before now. A voice whispered in Naomi's ear that that could be one of the many reasons Lillie had been so pissed. Had Naomi known that Lillie had needed her help, she would have made it a priority to help her first, before any other; but Naomi hadn't *seen*, hadn't known, and she blamed nobody but herself for the slip, for she had been blinded, too blinded by the world around her to see what was so close to her, so close that she hadn't seen it at all.

# CHAPTER EIGHTEEN

Back at the abandoned asylum, Naomi wandered from room to room, attempting to connect with an elusive past. Just like the first time she had visited, she had been trying too hard. She knew it but didn't know what to do *about* it.

Barry's trial loomed overhead, and Naomi knew justice would be served. She had stood here and helped to provide closure for that case. Now she just needed to concentrate and do the same for Lillie.

Still nothing. Damn–Bryce was in her head, clouding it with his face, his voice, his presence, and his absence. *Remember,* Naomi told herself. *Remember, without helping Lillie, you can't find your way back to Bryce.*

Darkness crept into the room before Naomi felt the shift of energy in the air. She held her breath for what was to come next. Knowing already what the impending vision would take out of her, she was equipped with a bottle of water and some ibuprofen.

"Lillie?" Naomi cried out to the stained walls. "Lillie? Where are you?" She closed her eyes, clearing her thoughts, which proved a much easier job now, knowing Lillie was here with her in this room.

*"Bobby? Bobby, it's safe. Come in."*

*The teenage boy's eyes darted around, behind him, then in front of him, scanning the room. He pocketed the key that he had used to enter Lillie's room.*

*"It's okay. They're all gone. Only the nurses at the front desk are still here. They won't come looking again. They already found me sleeping an hour ago." Her wicked grin widened, and the boy's shoulders visibly relaxed.*

*"Tonight's the night. Are you ready?"*

*Naomi scanned the small room, taking note of a pillowcase filled with what must be the only items that belonged to Lillie. She noticed that Bobby held a small pillowcase as well.*

*"I—I'm not sure about this. I have a bad feeling."*

*"You and your bad feelings. Bobby. Tonight is perfect. We have to do it."*

*"I don't know that I can."*

*"You don't believe me, then? Don't you want to save them? It's the only way. I can't stay here one more minute, knowing that they need me. I've seen what's going to happen. I feel it will be tonight, and if you don't help me, their blood will be on your hands."*

*She was so convincing, Naomi thought as she watched a young Bobby turn his hands around, searching for the proverbial blood.*

*"Okay, Lillie, okay." He turned behind him, eyes glued to the door. "Let me just check once more to make sure they're not watching."*

"All they do is talk, talk, talk. I hear them whenever I press my ear to the door. I hear them now. Let's go!" Lillie hissed.

"What if they catch me?"

"They haven't noticed the missing key yet, right? If we wait any longer, they just might."

"But what if they won't allow me to wander about in the daytime? They trust me to have that bit of freedom."

"Freedom that I don't have, freedom Joshua and his family don't have. It's a small sacrifice on your part for something better, something bigger."

Oh, Lillie. Naomi nearly cried out.

Such as wise, wise, girl.

She found herself wishing for a moment that she could have had the privilege of knowing her relative in life. It struck Naomi that she no longer referred to Lillie as a tyrant or monster. The ice in Naomi's veins had started to melt when she thought of Lillie, and her purpose for helping this child took precedence over everything, including, at the moment, Bryce.

"All clear," Bobby whispered, his blue eyes wide with fear. He opened the door delicately, nodding for Lillie to follow.

Clutching her pillowcase, Naomi saw hope cross Lillie's small features, and like a movie to which you already know the outcome, Naomi prayed for an ending she knew wouldn't come.

"This way," Bobby said, creeping down the dimly lit hallway. They walked together, Bobby reaching for Lillie's hand as they approached the door to what must be the stairway—the way out.

"Stop," Lillie spat out in a whisper. "Look." A nurse approached from far down the hallway, head slumped as she hummed softly to herself. Lillie pulled his hand toward the nearest door, which turned out to be a small storage closet.

Naomi's heart thumped in time with Lillie's and Bobby's. She sucked in her breath as she waited for the footsteps of the nurse to pass from outside the small closet.

"It's okay, Bobby. We're safe." Lillie, apparently once quite the nurturer, held the older boy in her arms and soothed him, not unlike the way she had done with Joshua in the passageway. Naomi's eyes swelled with tears as she witnessed a young girl who was ahead of her time. Had she been given a chance to grow up and become a woman, she was sure Lillie would have been a trendsetter for all women to aspire to. Naomi's soul shouted for Lillie to succeed, felt such pride at being related, however distant, to this amazing little girl.

"Tell me that story about Duchess," Bobby whimpered. "Tell me something normal, something good."

As they waited out the footsteps of the nurse and then several minutes beyond, just to be on the safe side, Lillie soothed a shaken Bobby with one of her favorite tales, the one in which she had met Zelda, or rather, Duchess.

"I was alone in my world with parents who never understood me. I had Joshua and his family, of course."

Joshua. Upon hearing her speak of the little boy from the stairway, Naomi's heart melted.

"And one day, the most wonderful man arrived from the New England States and moved in right down the path from us. My mother seemed charmed by him, calling him a wise, wandering soul. She and father had him over for tea, for supper, and each time he came to visit, he brought Duchess, and he told us of the most romantic tales of his one true love, a woman named Adelia, who had met her fate in an isolated lighthouse by the sea. He hoped to love again, and I have to believe he will."

"What was his name again?"

"Devon. Devon Bane."

"That's right. Go on, Lillie, but be quiet, please."

"Devon would laugh as Duchess always found her way to

my house, and eventually he gave in, told me that the heart wants what the heart wants—what he meant was that Duchess wanted to be with me." She paused as a faraway look came over her eyes, and a smile lit up her face. "That was okay with me because I wanted her too. My heart wanted Duchess."

Naomi choked up with emotion, tears flowing freely down her face.

"Oh, Lillie." She clutched her chest as she listened to Lillie chatter on in her whisper of a voice about her friendship with Duchess. Finally, they must have thought the coast was clear, for Lillie opened the door and peeked her head out.

"It's safe." She led the way now, escorting Bobby down the hallway to the stairwell door.

"Are you coming with me?" Lillie's eyes searched Bobby's face. "I don't know."

"Come on. You'll come with me and stay with me once I save the family. You said you wanted to. You don't even have parents to go home to."

An orphan. Naomi nearly mouthed the word. And then she wondered exactly what Lillie must have told him regarding the slaves trapped in her passageway. Didn't he wonder why, all these years later, slaves would still be on the run? Maybe she hadn't mentioned the detail that Joshua and his family were slaves, or maybe he just didn't want to know—maybe he just wanted to please her. Maybe he was simply mesmerized by this little girl who set herself apart from others in an undeniable way.

"What is that?" A cry could be heard from somewhere down the hallway. A nurse. It had to be one of the nurses approaching. "Who's there?"

"Go," Bobby ordered, his tone firm. "They'll catch us, and you'll never get to save that family."

The nurse's calls became more insistent. "Go, Lillie."

Lillie's eyes strained with pain. "Please, Bobby, you said…"

"There's no other way. They'll search the building. You need this time to escape."

"Bye, Bobby." Lillie pressed his hand before releasing it, then she grabbed him and embraced him one last time. "I'll never forget you and all you've done for me."

"Go, and Lillie?" He hesitated just one last second.

"Yes?" Her eyes held a sliver of hope.

"Hug Duchess for me?"

Lillie nodded through her tears and then, without glancing back, fled for the stairwell. As Naomi watched Lillie's retreating form sprint down the stairs, she heard Bobby explaining to the nurse that somehow his door must have been unlocked and that he must have been sleepwalking.

Before she had a chance to wonder if Bobby would forever be an orphan locked behind these walls, she caught sight of Lillie as she opened the side door of the building, her blonde hair flowing as she ran for the woods on the darkest of nights.

# CHAPTER NINETEEN

*F*ROM THE DARKNESS *outside the old hospital, to the isolated midnight streets of a small New York state town, she ran with purpose toward her destination. Naomi followed Lillie every step of the way, rooting for a soul destined to fail, but cheering for her, nonetheless, with every ounce of her being.*

*When Lillie entered her home, she didn't go to search out her parents, rather she seemed to steer away from them as she made her way to the back of the kitchen, right behind the stove.*

*She paused, briefly, and gazed around the dark room. "Tsk, tsk," she called out.*

*Duchess appeared in a flash, and Lillie expelled a breath of relief, scooping the cat into her arms before pushing at the door.*

*She pushed, a bead of sweat trickling down her chest— shoving her body against a door that had recently been sealed tight. She located the nails and nearly screamed in frustration. They couldn't do this. They couldn't.*

She wouldn't allow her parents to stop her from fulfilling the most important mission of her young life. She couldn't wake her parents—couldn't ask them for help, so she did the next best thing and ran for her father's shed.

Lillie flew toward the shed, Duchess a mere step behind her. The distinct howl of a pack of wolves beyond caused her to pause briefly and shiver, but she would not allow herself to be spooked by the ominous call of the creatures she feared most.

Once she had the shed in sight, she pounced on the door, rushing inside to throw tool after tool to the side.

Naomi watched as she threw garden tools, an ax, and metal shears to the side.

"Please, please, please." Lillie spoke aloud, tossing tools to the floor. In desperation, she rummaged through the last metal box, finding some type of iron rod that looked promising.

Feet flying, the blonde girl swept through the grass, her pace increasing as she made it back to the house with Duchess by her side.

With determination Naomi could have never dreamed possible, Lillie pried at the door, time and time again, sweaty, crying silent tears, until she freed the doorway. She turned to pick up Duchess then dropped the tool under the stove. She gently placed Duchess inside the passageway then attempted to fix the doorway the best she could and pulled the stove with all her might, finding power and strength from inside her. It was the best she could do—she figured it would cover her tracks. No one would be the wiser, and she had her way out up top. She called out and then disappeared beyond the dark walls of the ill-fated passageway.

"I'm here, Joshua. I'm here!"

Naomi's heart was in her throat as she knew the scene that would inevitably play out again just as it had so many times before. Hadn't Lillie realized that she was too late? Many, many years too late?

It appeared that she had no clue that what she had witnessed many times wasn't a vision, wasn't a premonition, but rather the past playing itself out in the cruelest trick of nature. Naomi could only watch a patient Lillie wait out the appearance of the family that would soon materialize. It must have been hours later, for Naomi could hear the policemen searching the home and cringed as Lillie grew quiet, hushing Duchess as one of the men noticed screws on the floor, but instead of searching the passageway, he whistled and returned with a hammer to seal the entrance shut once more. He must have been bored, figuring he was helping out, not knowing that beyond the walls lay a passageway holding the lives of two souls Naomi loved so deeply.

A determined Lillie whispered to Duchess not to worry, that they had their way out upstairs.

All Naomi could do was scream out the words she knew Lillie couldn't hear, telling her to yell, to pound on the door the policeman had yet to walk away from.

"Listen, you have to come with me, all of you." Lillie stood right in front of them, but only Joshua appeared to see her.

"Something's wrong, Maribel, I feel it."

"They'll let us know when it's safe, they will. They're good people."

"We're not going to get out of here alive. I love you. Remember that, my beautiful wife." Another whisper.

"What is the matter with you? Now stop that nonsense. You're scaring the heck out of yourself and me. Now drink that water and hush." She handed her husband a dirt-stained cup.

"Mama?" The boy turned his tear-stained face toward his mother. "Do you see her?" The woman passed the water to her son.

"See who?"

"Her. It's Lillie again."

"You must be delirious, talking about that girl again. Now drink that water."

"She makes me feel better, helps the pain go away," the boy said, holding out his hand for Lillie to grasp.

"Joshua," Lillie stated with a firm conviction. "It'll be different this time, I promise, if only you'll get your mother and father to listen to me."

"No, they won't, and it won't do any good anyhow." Joshua wept into his dirt-stained smock.

"I unlocked the top floor doorway, before I left—come on. We have to go," Lillie wailed, her high-pitched shriek piercing through Naomi.

"It's not true. We tried it already, Lillie. Don't you see? Someone sealed it tight."

"No, it's not possible." Lillie ran to the top floor at the speed of lightning. She pushed, shoved, and slammed her body against the doorway over and over, in an endless quest to change history.

Still not giving up hope, Lillie ran back to Joshua and grabbed hold of him. "I'm here, and I'm not going anywhere. I have you, you hear. Now hold on tight."

Now, she distracted the boy and his weeping parents with a lullaby, Lillie's own sorrow barely contained as a tear spilled out and traveled down her cheek.

Just like the times before, Naomi heard the shout of men's voices and the screaming from a woman and man below, right in the kitchen.

"Run! Run!" But she already knew the outcome of this scene that played out so cruelly before her.

Shots rang out from as a woman's shrill scream sounded from below.

*Lillie held the wailing boy's hands and then pulled him impossibly close as the men lifted their rifles and aimed. Lillie then turned, locking her hopeless eyes with Naomi. "It always goes like this." Lillie's body then slumped forward with the weight of the family, like dominoes, falling against her, never breaking contact with the dying boy.*

*Naomi screamed out loud for all the pain and sorrow they had suffered. When would it end?*

*"They're gone. Gone. They're all gone," Lillie wailed uncontrollably as she rocked the boy back and forth, his eyes forever frozen in fear.*

*"It always ends this way."*

A river of tears slid down Lillie's face as Naomi sunk to the floor of the deserted asylum, placing her hands on her head in anguish for the little girl, the family that had lost their lives, and for her own family, for it was lost as well.

In the past, the vision would stop at Lillie's sorrowful last words of finality for Joshua and his parents. This time, she was granted more.

Lillie had sat for what had seemed like hours but what Naomi soon came to discover was that it had actually been days, clutching Zelda. Girl and cat, together in their sorrow for lost friends, together in the last moments of their lives, their bond forever sealed.

Naomi saw flashes of the series of events that had sealed both Lillie's and Zelda's fate.

*"What did you see? Do you know anything?"*

*Bobby's eyes filled with fear, and Naomi knew he wouldn't*

give up Lillie's whereabouts right now, not with the plan for Lillie to save an already doomed family.

"You were her friend. Tell me—where would she go?" Lillie's mother's face came into view—again, the shock of seeing what appeared to be a mirror image of herself stole Naomi's breath.

"I don't know for sure, ma'am, but she always spoke of running away, finding a new home in one of those orphanages south of here—you know, the one that takes children and finds them better homes."

"But—that's ludicrous. It's miles from here. How would she even find it?" Lillie's father buried his hands in his hair and searched the doctor's face for answers.

"She's a very resourceful little girl," the doctor muttered, looking away from Lillie's parents.

*Oh, if only they knew.*

"How could you let this happen?"

"What kind of place is this?"

"Did she ever speak of trying to come back home? We could go back and wait?" Lillie's mother grabbed Bobby's shoulders, shaking him.

"No—she was—quite upset with the two of you. I think it's the last place she'd go." Bobby stated, his firm words settling in around all of them.

"What have we done?" Lillie's mother cried out, the weight of her body falling onto her husband. "What have we done?"

"We'll find her, dear. The police are on their way."

Unfortunately, a young child fitting the physical description of Lillie was seen wandering alone, hair and clothes unkempt. The location of her whereabouts was close enough to arouse suspicion that it could be Lillie, so the destination of the search excluded a more thorough search of Lillie's home; instead, Lillie's parents and the policemen found themselves following a trail of despairing bread crumbs toward a child who bore such a striking resemblance to Lillie but wasn't her. It had taken them over five days to search—five days that Lillie's parents had stayed with a relative who lived in the area. Once they had finally located this child, she ended up being a lonely orphan, searching helplessly for a better life, one that didn't include the verbally and physically abusive hand of her foster family. It was, unfortunately, the perfect storm.

The police had monitored the area of Lillie's home with the occasional presence of an officer—one instructed to keep an eye on the outside of the home with an occasional sweep of the inside.

At first, Lillie would cry out, bang on the doorway behind the stove, screaming for her life. She had made sure the top doorway was open—how could her parents have done this? But she knew—her mother didn't wish for her to chatter on and on about a family, one whom her mother couldn't see—couldn't understand. Her parents had thought that if they sealed both doorways, they would put a lid on her incessant talk of a family whom only Lillie could see. They had no idea that by doing so, they had forever shut both Lillie and Duchess off from the rest of the world.

Duchess stayed loyal and brave until the very end, pressing his frail body against Lillie's own weakened frame.

Naomi couldn't bear the crushing pain of watching the stages that had taken both Lillie and Duchess from the world—from denial, to panic, to a false sense of hope—Naomi watched until Lillie and Duchess came to terms with their grim situation, clinging to one another through Lillie's tears.

In the end, Lillie put on a brave face, her voice barely audible. "It's going to be okay, Duchess," she choked out her words into the dusty space before them. "They'll come for us, any minute now." Lillie's voice trailed off as she closed her eyes and *then opened them one more time. Duchess's shallow breathing eventually slowed until she opened her own eyes and rubbed her head against Lillie's.*

*"I love you, Duchess," Lillie managed, her arms still around her beloved cat. "I love you."*

*Together, they held on to that last moment, and together, they closed their eyes, bonded in death as they had been in life.*

# CHAPTER TWENTY

Naomi didn't recognize the sound of her own sharp wailing as she cried out for Lillie and Duchess. Her heart couldn't take any more–she broke, her emotions overruling her body and her mind as she screamed, melted to the floor, and prayed for this little girl who was coming to mean so much to her.

It didn't end there. As if she hadn't witnessed enough pain, she opened her eyes to find the scene unfold around her, sucking her into the last place on earth she wished to be.

*"What happened here? Someone has been here, going through my tools!"*

*Lillie's mother raced to the house, her husband and a police officer one step behind her.*

*The mother must have put it all together, as she sprinted for the kitchen and cried out when she shoved the stove to the side.*

*"She's in here–she's in here! Lillie!"*

"Lillie!" Her father shoved his way up the stairs, practically knocking his wife over in attempt to reach his daughter. "She's there up top. I see her!"

They found out seconds later, as the father scooped Lillie's limp body into his arms...they were too late, too late to change the fate of the bravest little girl Naomi had ever met.

Turning her face away from Lillie, Duchess, and her parents, Naomi closed her eyes, but she couldn't silence the sobs of Lillie's parents, a sound she would never erase from her mind.

Had Lillie ever seen this part of the night unfolding? Had she seen the love, the remorse, and the regret shining in their tears? Or had she blocked it all out, out of anger, bitterness, and resentment?

"Look," Naomi commanded, knowing Lillie must be somewhere close. "I have a lesson for *you*—it's *your* turn to open your eyes and see—see the love, see how heartbroken your mother and father are—for you. They only did what they could, what the doctors recommended."

A tug from her shirt caught Naomi's attention and she wept aloud. "Lillie!" Lillie held Duchess in one arm and then clutched Naomi's hand in her other.

"Watch," Naomi instructed, her eyes shining with tears as she and Lillie watched her parents hold her lifeless form and pray for Lillie's love and forgiveness.

"They love you. They hadn't known any better—didn't understand your gift."

Words didn't come for Lillie, but hope sprang to life in her eyes and slowly lit her face into the most beautiful smile Naomi had ever seen. Light radiated around Lillie and Naomi knew—she *knew* she was on borrowed time with both Lillie and Duchess.

She would never have been prepared to say goodbye to

Zelda, to Duchess. How would she go on without her cat? The cat she had found and the cat who had led her here, precisely where she needed to be—all tangled up with the lost souls—the lost souls who had now been found.

"You did it, girl." Naomi wept freely as Lillie nodded her approval and placed Duchess in her arms for one last time. "You did your job, Duchess. You brought me to Lillie." She kissed the cat, smothering her with wet kisses. Duchess howled with sorrow, pressing her body as close to Naomi as was possible. "We may have veered off the beaten path a few times, but I wouldn't have had it any other way."

She thought of Maggie, Ryan, and Nick, and although Lillie had been impatient at waiting for her one true blood connection, the only one who shared the unique gift of "seeing," Naomi knew that those three other souls had most definitely been part of her destiny as well.

With a move that Naomi never thought she would have to make, she kissed the top of her cat's head and handed Duchess back to Lillie for good. Lillie clung to Naomi for a long moment before speaking.

"I'm sorry it took so long for me to see, to see what was right in front of my own face."

"One of your lessons." Naomi nearly laughed through her thick tears. And suddenly, Naomi realized that the lessons Lillie had once placed upon her weren't lessons from cruel parents. Rather they were lessons Lillie, herself, had punished herself with.

"Thank you, thank you, Mother."

Naomi nearly gasped at Lillie's error.

"I'm sorry. You just look so much like her."

"I know."

"I wanted to tell you that one day you'll be a good mother

yourself, the best." Lillie gazed up at her, eyes brimming with tears.

Not too long ago, Lillie had taunted her about not being a *real* mother–now this. She realized just how far they had come.

"Thank you. That means so much to me, Lillie." She ruffled her blonde hair, smiling down at her and Duchess. "You take care of each other, okay?" Naomi's eyes searched both of their faces, seeing the white light glow more fluorescent by the moment.

"You go to them–go to Bryce and Holly."

If only it were that easy. She knew that the battle with Bryce wasn't over yet. He wouldn't be satisfied with the fact that the spirit of Lillie was now settled because he would just wonder who or what was coming next.

As if Lillie read her mind, she shook her head and squeezed Naomi's hand one last time. "They're gone–we're all gone from here."

Naomi turned her head to glance around the room. "You mean–?

"All gone. From your home, that is. You can be alone with your family–if you choose to," Lillie said.

"Choose to?" But Naomi understood. She would always have Maggie, Ryan, Nick, and now Lillie and Zelda, but if she wished to make her family work, to truly be a part of it, she needed to focus all of her energy on Bryce, Holly, and hopefully, someday, a new baby.

"Your purpose here has been fulfilled. It's time to let go, time to live your own life," Lillie said. "If you choose."

Naomi knew she would always have a tie to these spirits, but knowing that her job was done, helping these wonderful souls? A chill came over the room. Naomi felt a prickle flicker across the back of her neck as she looked across the room. There, within the cold, dark walls of the asylum stood Maggie, Ryan, his sister, Raegan, and Nick. In a moment's time, the room filled with a warmth she had never experienced–warmth, incredible light, and love. Naomi couldn't tear her eyes from Ryan, for he had been one of her best friends. His lips moved, silently pleading with her to let them all go.

"You can do it, Naomi, you're strong." Lillie glanced up at Naomi, her eyes sprinkled with tears. "You look just like her, you know? You look just like my mother."

The two turned toward the light, which grew brighter from across the room. There. Naomi could see Lillie's mother and father, and then she saw Joshua clutching onto both his parents, waiting for Lillie amongst the others, smiles finally etched upon their faces. It was time.

"Goodbye, Lillie. Goodbye, Duchess." She lifted her hand to her mouth, covering her sobs.

"Wait–I have one last lesson for you, Naomi. Lesson number ten: appreciate what you have, and never let the ones who matter most in this world, the ones you love, get away."

She choked back her words and knew none were really needed. She knew exactly what Lillie meant, and her heart overflowed with love for not just Bryce and Holly, but for Lillie and Zelda, and all the souls that had been entangled so beautifully with her own.

"Mother?"

Naomi looked down at Lillie, ready to answer, but realized Lillie hadn't been speaking to her. She had been gazing at her actual mother across the room. At this moment, Naomi realized she had come to think of Lillie as a daughter and knew, in a way, she always would.

"Go, it's time Lillie."

Lillie held Duchess tight, took a step toward her parents, a step toward the light, then stopped and retreated back to her, slamming her body against Naomi.

"I love you," Lillie cried out with a fierce hug, clinging to her, wet tears pressing against Naomi's waist.

"I love you, too." She watched as Lillie broke free, Zelda in tow, and ran toward her parents. When Lillie had finally reunited with her mother and father, Naomi gazed at all of them, and knew the power of true love, knew the power of family.

She also knew what she had to do.

# CHAPTER TWENTY-ONE

"I NEED TO speak with you," Naomi uttered the words she had practiced saying in her head since she arrived back home. What if he said no? That he had already made up his mind? She held her breath, waiting out his response.

"Naomi–"

"Please, Bryce. Just hear me out. Things have changed. I only need a few minutes, and then, if you want to leave, be my guest." She hoped that he wouldn't.

"I–oh, damn, Naomi." She imagined him, running a hand through his thick, brown hair, pacing.

"Please." The word came through in a desperate whisper.

"A few minutes, that's all. I have to pick up Holly at her friend's house."

"You got it." She pumped her fist in the air, thankful for at least a chance to get him to understand. She needed to see his face, read the expression in his eyes for this conversation.

He hung up the phone, saying he would be over in about a half an hour. It would give her time to plan but also time to freak out. Again, what if he had decided that although he loved her, he and Holly were better off without her. She might not be able to prove that Lillie had changed and was gone for good, but she had to try.

As she paced the floor, she considered her plea and then decided that she would wing it, speak from the heart. When she heard the knock, she walked toward the door, wondering how Bryce had gotten off work so quickly.

"Where the hell have you been?" Miriam barked the second she opened the door.

"Um–I've been kind of busy." She gave Miriam the short version, promising to fill her in later with the details.

"Whoa–I mean–whoa."

A speechless Miriam was a rarity. She almost laughed, but her tension about Bryce's visit reined her in.

"I know."

"And? Have you thought about this? I mean really thought about what it will mean to you to leave them all behind?"

Hearing Miriam gave her pause; there was such finality to the words. But it wasn't as if she'd never see visions of her beloved souls in her dreams, and she knew from time to time, they might even show their faces. But her job of helping the new, desperate lost souls would be finished, and the thought, though unsettling, was nothing in comparison to imagining her life without her family.

"The way I see it, it's a no brainer," Naomi exclaimed, her eyes wide.

Miriam crushed her in a hug, holding on for a moment longer. Was Miriam sniffling? She pried herself from her friend's arms and laughed, then cried, right along with her.

"Don't make me all mushy before he comes over. I'm a wreck as it is." Naomi sniffed, wiping her hands under her eyes,

"You got this. You hear? He'd be a fool not to want you."

"He'd also be a fool to stay."

"Don't you ever say that again. You'll be fine. You both will, and no, he'd be crazy to walk away from you. You're different, Naomi, on a completely different plane from the rest of us. I'd date you myself if I weren't straight." Miriam laughed aloud and hugged Naomi again before walking toward the door.

"I'm sorry, I completely forgot to ask how you and Cole were doing."

"Me and Cole?" Miriam showed her poker face, one she took to a whole new level.

"Don't even pretend with me. I'm your best friend. I can see right through your bullshit."

Miriam grew serious, her eyes drifting to the floor. "I don't know. I mean I'm not sure I can let myself go through the pains of dating, getting to know someone, when chances are it'll just go south."

"Why would you even think that?" But she knew why and regretted her choice of words. Phil had done a number on her. She'd already had trust issues stacked a mile high before he had used her and spit her back out.

"Don't—"

"Miriam," Naomi began, "in your own words, he'd be a fool to let you go."

"Just do me a favor?"

Naomi nodded, already knowing Miriam was closing the door, building up her wall on the conversation. She only hoped Miriam wouldn't close Cole out. It was the happiest she had seen her friend since before Phil.

"Yeah, I get it. I'll leave you alone."

"Thank you."

Miriam walked back to her house, and Naomi made a mental note to check her friend's house tonight, to see if Cole's truck would be in the driveway.

*Don't screw this up.*

She watched her friend retreat into her home and then sighed, her worries back to the present, back to Bryce. Normally she would grab Zelda and hold her, whispering her thoughts to her cat, thinking the whole time there wasn't a chance Zelda understood a word she mumbled to her. And now, she missed Zelda terribly, even knowing she was where she rightfully belonged. She could only hope Zelda would take it upon herself to make an appearance from time to time.

But Lillie's words had rung with goodbyes, of choices. Who knew, though? Who really knew the possibilities and the "rules" of this other realm?

"Naomi?" Bryce knocked on the screen door, startling her. Damn, he looked good–tired, sad, but so good.

It took every ounce of restraint on her part not to jump into his arms, fast-forward this conversation to where they were past this–to a place where all was well. Unfortunately, they had work to do in order to repair their relationship–she only hoped he was willing to put in his share.

"Come in, sit." Naomi cringed at her cordial, formal words.

He *lives here. He lives here.*

This was wrong, so wrong that she had to invite her husband into *their* home, invite him to sit on *their* couch.

She watched the weariness on his face as he sat down.

"Would you like something to drink?"

He stood back up and placed a hand on Naomi's wrist. "Stop. Just sit down. You said we need to talk, so let's talk."

Her stomach dropped. This was it. It was either going to happen or not, and she was powerless to do anything but tell him the facts and wait to see how he would react. It sucked feeling powerless.

"Okay." They both settled on the couch, but she kept a painfully respectful distance from him. Her hands shook as she started to speak. He grabbed hold of them, stilled them, and it gave her the courage to start.

"It was her all along–Lillie, I mean. Lillie and I, we go way back. Way, way, back…"

She explained her history, not leaving out one bit of the story. His eyes held hers, he gulped as she spoke, but never once did his eyes leave hers.

"Her gift–the one we share, it brought me to her, brought me to you. Even Zelda played a part in all of this."

At the mention of the cat's name, Bryce broke eye contact, his eyes searched the room for the cat that was never too far from sight. "Where is she? Is she okay?"

Naomi took a breath and continued. "She's more than okay, she's finally found Lillie, finally found the peace she deserves."

Bryce's mouth opened, agape at her words, and she could see him connecting the dots. He stood, paced the floor then returned to sit beside her. "Are you telling me–"

"Yup." She needn't say more.

"Naomi–"

"I know."

"I'm sorry." He placed a hand on her thigh. "I know how

much that cat meant to you."

"It's okay. I miss her like hell, but it's Lillie she belongs to, Lillie she needs to be with now."

He smiled, and she ached with the softening of his features. "It sounds like you've had a change of heart toward Lillie, huh?"

Her smile grew wider. "You could say that."

She told him of Lillie's mother, how similar they were, of the lessons, and then finally she told him about lesson number ten, her favorite lesson of all. "She said to hold on to your loved ones, to never let them go."

"Naomi–"

She held up a hand to silence him. "No, let me finish. They're done here–all of them. It was all part of my destiny, to be where I am with you, right here, right now. This is it–my reward, I suppose, of sorts. At least, that's the way I see it. Everything I've been through, every soul I've touched–it's all tied into you and me. And now, Bryce? Now we start over, now we make our own destiny."

She bit her lip, waiting for his response. "How can I be sure Holly won't be in danger again? How can *you* be sure?" But his eyes held hope, and she could see it growing by the second.

"Because I *trust her*, Bryce."

"And there won't be any others?"

"No, Bryce. She said I can be done with all of this, that they won't bother us here."

"Here?" His eyes grew wider as his hands pressed down on hers.

"They won't be here. She said we're clear–clear of any other roaming spirits in our home."

"But?"

"Well, as long as I've made up my mind to leave this part of my life behind, I'm in control. I make the decisions."

"And?" His warm smile broke through, and of course, as always, he seemed to read her mind.

"And I'm yours. I'm where I want to be, the *only* place I've ever wanted to be. Bryce, what I'm saying is, I'm all yours."

He cupped her face in his hands and pressed his warm lips down on hers, tasting her, feeling her for the first time in ages, or so it seemed. She opened her mouth to speak, but he silenced her with his mouth once more.

"What about Holly? Don't you have to pick her up?"

"Nah, I asked my dad if he would pick her up. Right now, it's you and me." He kissed her again.

"Is that so?" She laughed through her tears, hers mingling with the saltiness of Bryce's tears. She held him tightly for fear he would slip away from her again.

"Try me. You're not getting away from me ever again, Naomi." He took her hand, leading her up the stairs, to their bedroom. "Ever again."

"I can't wait to hug her. Did she miss me?"

"Are you kidding me? She only asked for you every five minutes of every single day."

She smiled at that, it was comforting knowing now that Lillie wasn't filling her head with evil thoughts of her, she and Holly would have a chance to reconnect, start over in a way.

Naomi frowned as they drove past Miriam's house. She hadn't seen Cole's car in the driveway at all today and after their conversation, it worried her.

"What's the matter?"

"Hm? Oh, nothing. It's just Miriam, I guess. She's got me a bit worried."

"Why? I thought you said she seemed happier than ever? I mean the few times I've seen her lately, that Cole guy has been there, and I thought she had finally met her match."

"That's the problem. She's getting cold feet. I hope he sticks around long enough to break through her force field."

"Ha. That's funny. She does kind of remind me of a superhero."

She had never quite thought of it like that, but he did have a point.

"I just hope she knows what she's doing."

"She's a big girl. She'll figure it out. You worry too much you know."

She twirled her hair around her finger, and he leaned over, placing his hands on hers. "Stop that."

"Yes, sir." She laughed, but her mind was still on Miriam. She would be okay, no matter what, but Naomi wanted her friend to open her heart and give someone all she had to give, without the fear of holding back.

They had driven in comfortable silence the rest of the way to Holly's grandparents' house. Naomi glanced at Bryce's handsome, boyish profile. She would never take this man for granted, she made the promise right then and there–a promise to hold onto him and Holly tightly and to never let them go. She swore she would never break that promise. Lillie had given a powerful last lesson, and she was an eager student.

"There she is." Bryce pulled up the driveway, careful to avoid Holly playing hopscotch with Bryce's mother. Her heart sank as she thought how Holly lost her playmate–she wouldn't play hopscotch or anything else for that matter, with Lillie anymore, a bittersweet thought for sure.

She pulled on her biggest smile as she opened the car door and then walked toward Holly.

"Mommy!"

Holly jumped into her arms as Naomi smothered her face in Holly's familiar strawberry scented hair. God, she smelled so good. She smelled like family. She smelled like home. She released Holly, holding her back to take a look at her.

"Want to play?" Holly turned to grab a small stone and then held her hand out to Naomi. Naomi reached for the stone and turned to look at Bryce. He nodded and smiled as he spoke to his mother, one eye on Naomi the whole time, like he couldn't bear to have her out of his sight.

They said goodbye to Bryce's parents, and she thanked them for all of their help. She knew that Bryce had filled them in on everything, and although his parents had seemed skeptical of her gift at first, she could sense that they were slowly coming around.

As they made their way up the small road toward their house, Bryce squeezed her hand then pointed at Miriam's house. "Look," he whispered.

Cole's SUV was in Miriam's driveway, snuggled in right beside hers. Maybe all would be okay with the world. She leaned slightly closer to Bryce and just enjoyed the moment.

GONE WERE THE dreams of torment–It had been weeks

since Lillie had left them, weeks since Nick and Lillie had finally relieved her of her nighttime terrors. In their place, she dreamt the sweetest dream of a baby, one who had Bryce's rich shade of brown hair and eyes just like his, but a smile identical to Naomi's.

In her dream, she held her infant daughter, kissing her head, rocking her gently. She gazed down into the girl's eyes, and instantly she knew–she knew this baby girl had a purpose, a reason for showing up in her dream. It was as if the baby also knew, for her wise eyes never left Naomi's face.

When she woke, she took care not to wake Bryce, she knew he had tossed and turned all night because she had as well. Placing a hand over her stomach, Naomi gagged, then ran to the bathroom, vomiting into the toilet.

Another flash and she gasped aloud. This time, her vision expanded across the room where Bryce sat on their living room couch. She sucked her breath in, unable to believe what played out before her eyes.

"What is it?" Bryce came padding down the hallway. "Naomi? Are you okay?"

She swiped at her mouth, gathering her composure. "Yeah, yeah, Bryce. I'm fine." But her hands shook terribly.

"Come back to bed." He grinned, pulling her hand.

She tried, but damn, that last vision stole her focus. Could it be true? The nausea rose again, and she sprinted to the toilet just in time.

"Are you *okay*?" Bryce approached her from behind.

"I will be."

"Will be?"

"I'll probably feel better in a few months." She tried the words out, liking how they sounded.

"A few *months*?"

She cracked a smile. "Bryce? You might want to sit down for a minute." Naomi took a moment to brush her teeth and rinse her mouth before continuing.

"What's the matter with you? Tell me." His face grew serious, and Naomi tried not to laugh.

Should she tell him just the facts? Or should she divulge what she *knew?* She could barely contain herself as she thought back to what she had just seen.

She led him back to their bedroom and waited until he sat beside her. There was no way to say it, other than to come right out with it.

"I kind of had a vision."

"Kind of?"

"Well, yeah. Are you ready to hear this?"

"Yes, go ahead."

"Remember when you told me you wanted a baby?"

His eyes widened and you could have heard a pin drop. "A baby?"

"Yes, um–"

"You saw it? You saw our baby?" His eyes widened, bright with expectation.

She nodded, barely containing the rest of her secret. She couldn't take it any more, not for one more second. "And Bryce? She had your eyes and hair, and my smile."

"Are you kidding me? Are you sure?" He grabbed her face, planting kisses over her entire face. She couldn't stop smiling as she considered her next words carefully before she spoke.

"Wait, Bryce. There's more."

"More? What could possibly top that? A baby who looks like a combination of the both of us."

"How about *another* baby girl? One with blonde hair

and blue eyes that appears to be the spitting image of Lillie?" She swallowed, watching his face transform from shock to what appeared to be joy. At least, she hoped it was.

"Are you okay? Are you happy?"

He lifted her off the bed and swung her in his arms, crying out to her. "Am I happy? Are you kidding me? Naomi, you've made me the happiest man in the world. You have no idea how happy I am." He placed her back on the ground and then kissed her firmly on the mouth.

"I love you, Naomi. I love you."

Lillie's face flashed before her, a grin set on her impish face. *"They'll carry on our legend."*

She gulped, imagining the magnitude of Lillie's statement. Two little girls caught up in ghosts, visions, and mayhem.

*Oh, Bryce. You're going to have your hands full.* She couldn't stop smiling at the thought.

"I love you, too."

As she kissed him, she thought she'd keep that last little part to herself–for now. After all, she had promised that *she* wouldn't bring any more spirits into this home. What their little girls may or may not do was another story, and her writer's mind figured someday it just might be that–another tale to be told.

### THE END

# ACKNOWLEDGEMENTS

I CAN'T BELIEVE the Maggie trilogy has come to an end. Although this series is over, you never know when a spin-off based on one of the supporting characters may appear. (My mind is already whirling with possibilities.) I've absolutely loved writing these unique characters; from Naomi to Lillie, and everyone in between. Each and every character holds a place in my heart.

Thank you to my amazing family. Mom, Dad, Alexandra, Alan, Jimmer, Damian, Amanda, and Siobhan–thank you for your continued love and support.

Thanks to all of my friends and a special mention to my longtime friends for many, many years of friendship and love–Janine, Jen, Jim, Karen, and Kim.

A big shout out to my street team; thank you for your help promoting and beta reading all of my novels and providing valuable feedback. Maari Hammond, Kallie Kennon, Cindy

Mathis, and Dawn Yacovetta, thanks for beta reading Lillie. Dawn Yacovetta, another big shout out for all the time you've spent helping out with my novels.

To my editor, Kathleen Payne, I love your attention to detail, your honesty, and how you encouraged me to put forth all my effort to make this novel the best it could be. It was wonderful working with you on this project and several others before.

Jill Sava, thank you once more for your help formatting, it's a pleasure working with you.

Lastly, I would like to thank my readers for their ongoing support. I hope you loved reading Lillie's story as much as I enjoyed writing it.

You can follow me at:
www.myaomalley.com
Instagram @myaomalley
Facebook.com/myaomalley

XOXO
Mya